PRAISE FOR

LIES MY GIRLFRIEND TOLD ME

"This book tenderly explores themes of loss and forgiveness.... **Peters capably addresses teen LGBT relationships** without making them the story's sole preoccupation." —*Publishers Weekly*

"In Peters's newest offering, questions of love and honesty abound.... This book does not focus on sexuality, and **it's a pleasure to read a typical teen romance that just happens to be between two girls**." —*SLJ*

"Peters has written another insightful, absorbing novel of relationships that is both emotionally and intellectually satisfying.... **This will have widespread appeal to both gay and straight readers** and is another strong offering from a well-established, popular author." —*Booklist*

PRAISE FOR

LUNA

A National Book Award Finalist
An Amazon 100 YA Books to Read in a Lifetime
An ALA Best Book for Young Adults
An ALA 2005 Stonewall Honor Book
A Lambda Literary Award Finalist

★"**Groundbreaking, finely tuned realism about a transgendered teen**.... Peters writes her characters with care and complexity." —*Kirkus Reviews*, starred review

"**Honest, heartbreaking, amazing**.... To this **mesmerizing drama**, Julie Anne Peters brings humor, intensity, and **an overwhelming sense of love and redemption**." —Jennifer Finney Boylan, author of *She's Not There: A Life in Two Genders*

"This novel breaks new ground in young adult literature with a **sensitive and poignant** portrayal of a young woman's determination to live her true identity and her family's struggle to accept Luna for who she really is." —*SLJ*

"The book is a **brilliant exposition** of the conflict, exaltation and terror involved in 'coming out' and I recommend it unreservedly." —Katherine Cummings, author of *Katherine's Diary: The Story of a Transsexual*, winner of the Australian Human Rights Award for Non-Fiction

"Shows [Luna's story] in such a realistic light that the reader will come away having learned something, and one might hope, with a **sympathetic attitude toward people dealing with gender issues**." —*VOYA*

"Peters' sensitive treatment of the struggles of the transgendered and those who love them **allows readers to see another aspect of the difficult adolescent journey toward identity** and the influence of societal pressure. Peters writes with **great empathy** and provides her readers with carefully chosen information about... the quest to become whole." —*KLIATT*

LIES my GIRLFRIEND told me

A novel by

JULIE ANNE PETERS

Megan Tingley Books
LITTLE, BROWN AND COMPANY
NEW YORK BOSTON

Little, Brown and Company
Hachette Book Group
1290 Avenue of the Americas, New York, NY 10104
Visit us at LBYR.com

Originally published in hardcover and ebook by Little, Brown and Company in June 2014
First Trade Paperback Edition: September 2017

The Library of Congress has cataloged the hardcover edition as follows:

Peters, Julie Anne.
Lies my girlfriend told me : a novel / by Julie Anne Peters.—First edition.
pages cm
"Megan Tingley Books."
ISBN 978-0-316-23497-9 (hardcover)—ISBN 978-0-316-23494-8 (electronic book)—
ISBN 978-0-316-36458-4 (electronic book—library edition) [1. Lesbians—Fiction. 2. Love—Fiction. 3. Grief—Fiction. 4. Secrets—Fiction. 5. Colorado—Fiction.] I. Title.
PZ7.P44158Li 2014
[Fic]—dc23

2013021597

ISBNs: 978-0-316-23495-5 (pbk.), 978-0-316-23494-8 (ebook)

Printed in the United States of America

LSC-C

10 9 8 7 6 5 4 3 2 1

This is dedicated to the ones I love.

Chapter 1

An earthquake shakes the ground beneath me and I swim to consciousness, grasping for a handhold. Mom's voice slithers into my dream state. "Alix? Honey?"

My eyelids flutter open to the faint light of dawn peeking through my window shade. "Alix?" she repeats.

I roll over and the clock comes into focus: 6:08. The alarm is set to go off in seven minutes. Why is she waking me?

A shadow looms in my doorway. Dad. Mom's sitting on the bed beside me. I get this sense of unease and push myself up on my elbows. "What's wrong?"

Mom takes my hand in both of hers. "There's been an accident." She glances over her shoulder at Dad. To me she goes, "A tragedy."

My stomach drops. "Is it Ethan?"

"No. Ethan's fine," Mom says.

I expel a sigh of relief. Over Christmas, right after he turned five months old, he came down with whooping cough. It was serious enough that Mom checked him into the hospital for two nights.

Dad comes into my room and sits at the end of my bed, rubbing my exposed ankle. It's weird. He rarely touches me.

"It's Swanee," Mom says. "She was out running this morning and collapsed. By the time anyone found her, she was gone."

"Gone?" What does that mean?

"She had a sudden cardiac arrest," Mom answers. "I'm so sorry."

"No," I say.

Mom presses my hand between hers. "There's nothing anyone could've done."

"I could've. I know CPR. You taught me."

She shakes her head. "A friend of mine in med school died of the same thing. He was playing soccer, not even running, just standing there waiting for the ball when his heart gave out. He was given CPR on the spot, but it was already too late."

"No." I hear my disembodied voice. "No, no, no."

Mom pulls me up and holds me, and then the screaming crescendos in my head: NO NO NO NO NO.

I have to see Swan. Get to her house and talk to her. I need to hold her, feel her lips on mine, her desire pulse through me.

Today's the day I'm going to tell her that I'm ready. She's been so patient with me while I've worked through my fear. It frustrated her. I know that. But now I'm ready to take our relationship to the next level. "No more waiting," I'll whisper in her ear as soon as I see her.

My head is clouded and my mouth feels stuffed with cotton balls. Mom and Dad are gone from my room, so I drag myself out of bed and stagger to the bathroom. Unexpectedly, I hurl. Nothing in my stomach. I dry heave three more times.

I feel so weak I can barely hold my toothbrush, but somehow I manage to brush my teeth and start the shower. Standing under the massaging spray, I feel better. More alert.

I dress in jeans and a long-sleeved shirt and then grab my bag and Dad's car keys to drive to Swan's house. Mom's body barricades the door to the garage. "Where are you going?"

"To Swanee's. We're snowboarding at Keystone today. I told you." I told her last weekend. It's already February, and we've only been to the slopes three times this year. The first time during winter break, when Swanee and I met and officially became a couple.

"Honey, Swanee's gone. And today is Sunday."

Sunday? No, it's Saturday. "I'm late. We wanted to get an early start so we could get there before the lift lines got too long. I'll ask Jewell and Asher to follow me back to the house so I can drop off Dad's car, since they're coming, too—"

Mom clutches my arm. "Jewell and Asher need to make funeral arrangements. You can't go over there."

I push Mom away, hard. "Yes, I can." She catches her foot on a mud rug and stumbles backward into the washing machine.

"Alixandra!" She chases me to the garage, favoring the ankle she twisted when she tripped. "You're not going. They need to be with family now."

"I *am* family!" I yell. A dizzy spell makes me brace myself against Dad's Prius.

"You're in no shape to drive," Mom says. "Give me the keys."

Then it dawns on me. "You drugged me." I whirl on her and the vertigo makes my head spin. "You drugged me, didn't you?"

"I gave you a mild sedative, yes."

She drugged me because she knew what I was going to tell Swanee today. I don't know how, but she knew.

"Swanee is dead." Mom clutches both my arms. "She's gone, Alix. She died yesterday morning."

"I don't believe you."

Mom looks hurt. "I'd never lie to you."

The statement makes me reel, considering all the lies I've told her lately.

My right hand is trembling, but I manage to get the key in the lock and open the door.

Mom blocks me from getting in.

"I have to go!" I shout at her. My voice lowers a notch. "I *have* to."

She gazes into my eyes. "You can't drive. You can hardly stand, and you don't even have shoes on."

I peer down and see she's right.

"Do you have your cell?" Mom asks.

My cell? Why? Is she going to take it away? Last month I overspent my text minutes, but what did Mom and Dad expect? I have a girlfriend now. We need to communicate.

She holds out her hand and I dig around in my bag for the phone. She plucks it from my palm and dials a number, looking at me while she waits for an answer. My toes curl under on the cold concrete.

What's the date? Swan's first track meet isn't until March, but she's been preparing all year.

Run. She's a runner. She's tall and lean, not an ounce of body fat. I feel like a blob next to her. Swanee has a good chance of winning the 5A title again this year for Arvada. She has six offers on the table from the top track-and-field colleges. She doesn't want to go out of state and leave me behind, but I told her she has to follow her dream. So she signed with Arizona State. It's going to be hard carrying on a long-distance relationship for a whole year. We can do it, though. Until I get to Arizona, our love will see us through.

Mom's talking to me.

"What?"

"Give me the keys."

I fist them behind my back.

She says, "Jewell wants to see you. But please, Alix, show respect. She has to make arrangements for Swanee."

No. Jewell will greet me at the door like always. "Hi, Alix." She'll hold the door wide open for me. "Wassup, girlfriend?"

And I'll tell her. She might make a cappuccino for me and sit at the kitchen table to shoot the breeze. She's so great. Eventually, she'll say, "Swan's in her room. Go on in." She's fine with me being in Swanee's room with the door closed. Swanee even said it'd be fine if I stayed over. My first thought was, How many girls have stayed over? But it was none of my business. I knew she wasn't a virgin, like me.

My mom would never let Swanee spend the night.

Horrors. We can't even be in my room together with the door closed. My parents are such prudes.

Mom stands there with her palm open, waiting for me to give up the keys. It's useless trying to hold my ground. I hand over the keys and she says, "Go put your boots on."

In the mudroom, I slip my numb feet into my boots.

It's snowing. When did it start to snow? Swanee hates it when the weather is crappy. It's enough to compete, she says, without having to freeze your ass off in snow or rain or sleet.

I know the route to the Durbins' by heart and direct Mom there.

In front of Swanee's house and around the cul-de-sac, there are ten or twelve cars parked. Mom pulls in behind Derek's van. Not Derek anymore. He wants to be known as Genjko. What a weirdo.

Mom says, "We'll just stay long enough to pay our respects, and then leave."

I race to the door. The thought of seeing Swan, of feeling the charge of electricity when our eyes meet and she smiles her love.

I ring the bell.

Swanee's sister, Joss, answers. I take one look at her and my breath catches.

"Who is it?" Jewell wedges herself between Joss and the door. Her eyes are puffy and red. She looks from Mom to me, hiccups, and says, "Oh, Alix." She covers her mouth and then smothers me in a hug.

It can't be true. It can't it can't it can't.

Chapter 2

I cry into my pillow all night. I cry as hard as Ethan used to when he was a newborn. That hopeless, helpless wailing. My cell's been ringing off and on, so finally I check the ID. It's an unknown number. I can't talk to anyone right now.

I don't even bother getting up for school. Mom doesn't make a big deal out of it, the way she usually does. She even asks if I want her to stay home with me. I tell her no. She has her job, her babies. She's a doctor in the neonatal center at St. Anthony where she keeps preemies alive.

Why? I wonder. So they can live until they're seventeen and then drop dead?

I cry. I must cry myself to sleep.

I'm awakened by a knock on my door. I roll over to see Mom stick her head in. "Joss is here to see you."

I want to say, Tell her to go away. I want to say, Can she bring back Swanee?

I feel a tear trickle out of the corner of my eye. It's 2:32. AM? PM? What day?

Joss plops on the edge of my bed. Her face is impassive, but I can tell she's struggling to maintain control. She and Swanee are only two years apart, and they're more like best friends than sisters.

A wave of resentment rises up inside me. All those years Joss had with Swanee, and I only got six weeks. Joss knows her better than I ever will. How fair is that?

She's dressed in black. She always dresses in black. Joss is one of those invisible moles no one ever notices. So unlike Swanee, who is bright and fun and lively.

Is. Was. I'm stuck in present tense.

Joss asks, "Why?"

Like I have the answer.

I wish she'd go. I can't engage with anyone right now, especially her.

"What are we going to do?" she says.

We? I know what I'm going to do. Lie here and die.

Swanee's only been dead for three and a half days. She could still come back, right? People can be resuscitated. People's hearts have stopped before, and doctors were able to restart them.

My mother could do it—if she wanted to.

Joss gets up, shuffles over to my dresser, and picks up my ski goggles.

GO! I want to shout. I want to push her out the door. I tuck my knees into my chest and turn over.

After about a year, she clues in. When she's gone, I just start bawling.

* * *

We met on a ski trip the Wednesday after Christmas. My BFF Betheny and I were in ski club at the time and had planned to go to Winter Park, but Betheny called that morning with bad cramps. Even though we'd already bought the lift tickets, I considered not going, since I hate doing things alone. Ethan was home from the hospital, and I should've asked Mom and Dad if they needed me to stay and help out. With chores. Not with Ethan. He scares me. He seems so fragile I'm constantly afraid I'll drop him or do something hideously wrong that'll damage him forever.

In the end, selfish me decided I deserved a break from the crying and coughing and sleep deprivation.

The ski bus was packed by the time I boarded. There was only one empty row, so I snatched it up. Most people from ski club I knew enough to smile and say hi to, but I sort of rode on Betheny's wings. She'd always been the popular one. She made the cheer squad this year, and even though we'd been friends since elementary, I sometimes felt totally outside her new flock of friends.

It wasn't her fault. I'm just insecure, I guess.

As I was digging out my nano, I heard, "Is this seat taken?"

I looked up and saw Swanee. My stomach did a double flip. Of course I knew who she was. Superathlete. Most out lesbian in school. I think every other gay and bi girl lusted after her from afar. At the beginning of the year she was with this girl Rachel Carter? Carver? Then I heard through the

Gay/Straight Alliance grapevine that Rachel had moved. I didn't know if they were still together or not.

"Hello?" Swanee said. "Sprekken zee Anglaise?"

"Huh? Oh, no. I mean, yes." Shit, I thought. Could I sound more dense? I moved my pack off the empty seat.

"You're Alix, right?"

She slid her pack under the seat in front of us while my mouth gaped open. "I'm Swanee," she said.

She knew my name. It nearly took a force of nature for me to breathe out, "Hi."

"A friend was going to come with me today, but she sprained her ankle," Swanee said. "Did we meet at Rainbow Alley?"

Rainbow Alley is Denver's LGBTQI Center. "I don't think so. I haven't been there in a while."

"Me neither. Oh, I know." She aimed an index finger at me. "You're in the GSA at school."

"Yeah." Even though I hadn't attended many meetings this year, since Betheny was always so busy and I still felt uncomfortable going alone.

"And you hang with the cheers." She sort of wrinkled her nose.

"Just one," I said. "Betheny. My best friend."

Swanee's eyebrows rose. "Is that all she is? Because everyone assumes..." The sentence dangled.

"What?" Everyone who?

She shrugged.

I might've let out a snort. Like a boar. "Betheny's not gay."

"You sure of that?"

"A hundred percent," I said. "She would've told me when I came out to her." In seventh grade. She was fine with it. In fact, she said she'd suspected as much.

Swanee held my eyes. Hers were so crystalline clear I felt like I was looking all the way to the bottom of the sea. "But do you like her that way?"

"No." I hoped the heat in my cheeks didn't register on the hot tamale scale. I'd wondered myself, and even fantasized about kissing Betheny. But it was only because I wanted so badly to find someone to love.

The bus rumbled off and Swanee sighed. I remember I couldn't stop peering at her in my peripheral vision. She had this long strawberry-blond hair with a streak of blue down my side. I'd asked Mom if I could highlight my hair, since it's this unremarkable shade of "dishwater" blond, sort of like splash back on your windshield after a snowmelt, and she said absolutely not, that I already had beautiful auburn highlights. I don't know where she was looking, but it wasn't in my mirror.

We weren't even to I-70 before Swanee sighed again and said, "I really hate skiing alone. Want to—"

"Yes." I cut her off.

She laughed and I about died of embarrassment.

We fell into an easy conversation, and by the time we were riding home, we were snuggling under a blanket and giggling our heads off.

I have to beg Mom—*beg* her—to let me stay home from school the rest of the week. Reluctantly, she agrees, but then makes it conditional on me babysitting Ethan if Dad has to go to the office. Dad's a Web consultant, so he works from home most of the time. I tell Mom, "No way." We have a stare-down and I win because I break into tears. I know Mom thinks it's all about Swanee, but it's more: What if Ethan realizes he's home alone with me?

"I only have one meeting with a client all week and it's today," Dad says, coming out of his office, "so I'll drop Ethan off at day care and leave the stroller."

I want to hug Dad. We don't hug in our family. "Thank you," I tell him.

He adds, "You'll need to walk over and pick him up by five. Can you do that?"

I sniffle and nod. He'll screech all the way home. I'll bring my nano.

Dad takes Ethan upstairs to pack diapers and stuff, and then they all leave. My stomach grumbles, reminding me I haven't eaten much since... I can't keep anything down. I toast a couple of frozen waffles and sit at the kitchen table. I think I'll call Swanee and—

I press my fingertips against my eyes and choke back a deluge of tears. How could she go and leave me like this? Without warning. No last words. What were the last words we exchanged? Friday night after school she had a track team meeting. She kissed me at my locker and said she'd see me in the morning for snowboarding.

That hardly counts. We talked more on Thursday, when we went to an open mic night. I was at her house, in her room, sitting on her bed cross-legged, watching her put on a shoulder-length, neon-blue wig and an all-black outfit like Joss would wear. Even though the shirt was oversize, I could see Swan's breasts and nipples. Sexy as hell. "How do I look?" Swan asked me.

I got off the bed to go to her and kiss her my answer. "Good enough to eat." I pretended to bite her neck and she went, "Ummm."

Joss muttered, "I'll meet you pervs downstairs," and left.

I said, "You could wear those ebony button earrings I made you."

Swanee sighed. "I would if I could find them."

Her room was worse than a hoarder's nest. Even though I bought her a jewelry box, she could never remember to put my earrings into it. If she could even find the box.

Swan said, "Anyway, I'm saving them for a special occasion." She ran her hands through my hair and, with that twinkle in her eye, murmured, "We'll play vamps later."

It was almost ten. Three bands were left to play, and I had to be home by eleven. Swanee said, "You're the only person in the world with a curfew that early," and Joss said, "What *is* a curfew?" They both howled.

My parents' rules and regs were so archaic.

Since she was a senior and I was a junior, Swanee and I didn't have any classes together, but we did eat during the same lunch period. For the life of me, I can't remember what we talked about on Friday. Trivia. Now I wish I had a recording of every word she ever said every moment of every day.

Saturday, I know, she got up early to run, the same way she does every morning. Did.

The end.

I feel myself losing it, so I slog up to bed, hoping to go to sleep for however long the grieving process takes. Forever?

My bedroom door flies open and Mom says, "Where's Ethan?"

Oh my God. I sit up and my brain slips a gear. "He's at day care."

She checks her watch. "They closed half an hour ago."

The door opens downstairs and I hear Ethan making his cranky/hungry sound.

"Thank heavens." Mom presses a hand against her chest. Dad clomps up the stairs and Mom takes Ethan from him.

Dad fills the doorway.

"I'm sorry," I say. "I fell asleep. . . ."

He looks at me just long enough to pierce my heart.

No. He has no right.

Swanee was like a psychic when it came to reading people, and she said she didn't like coming to my house because my parents always reeked of hater vibes around her.

Chapter 3

Mom says at breakfast, "The service for Swanee is Saturday at ten. There's no burial, since she's been cremated, but after the service Jewell and Asher are having an open house."

Cremated. I can't get past that word.

If her body was burned to a crisp, how will her heart ever be restarted? Can they even find your heart in soot?

Ethan slaps his high chair with both hands and Mom resumes feeding him baby slop.

I head up to my room.

"Alix?"

I ignore her.

"Alix!"

"What?" I swivel my head.

"I know this is hard for you," Mom says. "Jewell wanted me to tell you that this will be a celebration of Swanee's life, for as long as they had her."

That sounds like she won't be mourned. Or missed. How can anyone celebrate?

A volcano of hurt erupts in my gut and I sprint up the stairs to hurl.

The service is like no funeral I've ever been to, but then I've only attended one: my grandfather's, when I was six. I remember the organ music was sad. People murmured condolences to Dad and said what a pretty girl I was. I wasn't pretty because I'd been sobbing the whole morning. Grandpa was Dad's dad and my favorite grandpa. I cried so hard during the service, Mom asked if I needed to leave. I shook my head no; I didn't want to leave my grandpa. Dad gave the eulogy and not once did his voice even crack. Later, at the burial, he told us he wanted to stay a while, that he'd call Mom when he was ready. I looked over my shoulder on our way to the car and saw Dad with his head bent and his shoulders shaking. I wanted to run to him and squeeze him tight.

Swanee's service has a carnival atmosphere about it. There are balloon bouquets and teddy bears. A flowered arch. A banner with the words RIP, SWANEE that looks like everyone from school signed it, or attached a card to it.

The Durbins have hired a mariachi band, and they're playing "Livin' la Vida Loca," of all things.

We're late because Mom worked the night shift in the preemie ward. That, and I kept changing clothes, trying to decide. Or forestall. Not go. Not accept.

Mom finally had to come in and tell me, "We need to leave now, Alix."

I almost locked myself in the bathroom and told her to go without me. But I knew Swanee would want me there.

On the way to the service, we passed the Safeway, and my vacant stare wandered to our parking spot in back. What the hell...? Swan and I had discovered this gravel driveway that meandered into a copse of trees and then just ended. We'd park in her little pink Smart car and make out for an hour or so after school. Now the entire area's being razed. A bulldozer sat there, empty, but it had done its job of clearing the trees. Making way for apartments, or offices. Building the future.

I have no future.

Why didn't I just succumb to my desire for her? Every time I made her stop, I'd have to apologize. Over and over. Once, she asked, "Why won't you just let yourself go? I know you want me."

I said, "I do. But I need to feel this is forever."

"Alix, you can't be sure anything is forever." She drew a circle on my forehead with a slash through it, and then traced a heart on my chest. Like, Follow your heart and not your head. Stop thinking so much.

She was right about forever being meaningless.

At the church I can't help noticing all the red and white uniforms and letter jackets. Support from Swanee's teammates. I recognize faces of students, teachers, coaches, admins. Up front are the Durbins—Jewell, Asher, Genjko, Joss. Joss is sitting apart from the family, at the very end of the pew.

The band finishes "Livin' la Vida Loca" and the minister asks everyone to stand and pray. I can't believe Jewell and Asher are having a religious ceremony. They know Swan was anti-religion. Genjko's a Buddhist. He's shaved his head and taken a vow of silence. One time I walked by his bedroom door and caught sight of this shrine he'd set up with a gold-painted Buddha. He was kneeling in front of it, burning incense. When he saw me, he shot to his feet and slammed the door in my face. I asked Swanee what *Genjko* meant and she said, "Buddha's bitch." It cracked me up. I Googled the word and found out the real meaning is "original silence." Every time Swanee ran into Genjko, she'd make a thumbs-up sign and say, "Free Tibet, dude."

Swanee was a sworn atheist. So is Joss. I doubt Jewell and Asher go to church. I remember we did when I was young. And it got harder and harder for Mom and Dad to make me go. Early intuition? When I came out to myself, I realized how unwelcome I'd be in any Christian institution.

Where do atheists spend the afterlife? I want her to be... somewhere. I want to meet her there.

People get up and read or recite testimonials about Swanee. Jewell tells how Swanee was walking by the time she was seven months old, and could really book it. Jewell was forever chasing her down. "She was destined to be a runner," Jewell says. Her voice breaks and I feel my eyes welling. Jewell swallows down her tears. "She died doing what she loved most."

That was true. Every day she had to get her mileage in.

Asher talks about Swanee growing up, how she took to sports. She could totally kick his and Derek's butts at basketball. He doesn't say out loud that she is—was—gay. Swanee wouldn't be happy about that, either. She embraced her sexuality. I don't want to say she flaunted it, but she was never shy about showing me affection in the halls. Or anywhere. Except my house.

Asher has a surprise. He videotaped Swanee's last track meet, where she won the state title in the girls' 800 meter.

Joss jumps to her feet and races down the aisle.

I can't watch it, either. I get up and trip over people's feet all the way to the end of the row, and then head toward the exit. Joss is outside, leaning against the brick wall, lighting up a joint. Breathing hard, she takes a hit and offers the joint to me. I decline. If Mom or Dad smelled pot on me, they'd ground me for life.

Like it'd matter now.

The crowd at the Durbins' overflows into the backyard. It's a cold day, this ninth day of February. Gray clouds threaten snow. The Durbins have a long enclosed patio, and they've plugged in space heaters so people won't freeze. Still, I'm cold to the core. People sit or stand with paper plates of food, talking and laughing together. I don't think anyone should be laughing.

Mom and Dad are inside paying their respects, I suppose.

"Hey, Alix." A hand grasps mine. "We're all really sorry about Swanee." It's a guy from the GSA. A group of them have come together, dressed in their rainbow regalia. If they start to throw glitter, I'm out of here.

You know what? I'm out anyway. As I head for the gate, I almost collide with Betheny. She opens her mouth to speak and so do I. But I can't. I whirl and hurry inside to escape out the front door.

She has every right to despise me. It was my decision to drop out of ski club and mathletes. When you're in love, you naturally spend less time with your friends. But that's no excuse. I understood when Swanee asked me—or, rather, told me—I couldn't go to Betheny's birthday party last month. She didn't put it that way, but I could tell she was mad I was even considering it. Betheny should've known Swanee wouldn't be keen on the idea of me sleeping over, the way I always did. I'd be jealous, too, if Swanee was staying overnight with a girlfriend. Even a straight one, especially if everybody assumed...

"You don't need her," Swanee said. "You have me now. Anyway, cheers are all stuck-up sluts."

I wanted to say, Not Betheny. She's great.

But I didn't.

I should've called or texted Betheny to tell her I was sick or something. All I did was not show up. After her birthday, she stopped calling. Which was kind of a relief because it gave me an excuse not to call or talk to her. At lunch she wouldn't even look at me. But then she had her clique and I had Swan. So I guess all was right with the world.

On the Durbins' kitchen table and counters are casserole dishes and sandwich trays, potato salad, veggies and dip, tortilla rolls, shrimp rounds, mini quiches.

A voice sounds behind me. "I was hoping you'd get up at the service and talk about Swanee," Jewell says. "Maybe share some special memory?"

I try to smile at her. I want to explain that in our short time together we made so few memories that I don't have any I want to share.

"Eat," Jewell says. "Asher ordered enough food for an army."

"Jewell, the Zarlengos are here," Asher calls from the living room, and Jewell hustles off.

As I'm meandering through the crowd to let Mom and Dad know we can leave now, I sense movement behind me. Glancing over my shoulder, I see Betheny coming toward me. I duck into the back hallway. Damn. Someone's in the bathroom.

At the end of the hall is Swanee's room. The door is closed, but I feel her presence. She's waiting for me. I know when I open the door, she'll jump out and shout, "Surprise!"

She's such a prankster.

I twist the handle, push, and... nothing.

She is here, though. Her essence. I know this room so well: the clothes and shoes on the floor; the bed, dresser, desk, closet; the cacophony of colors on the walls. Smears of blue and green and purple over a bloodred base. We were going to repaint her room and she couldn't decide what color, so we were trying different samples. She never did decide. All her movie posters are still up. She was a Johnny Depp fangirl. She has pictures of him everywhere, movie posters from *Edward Scissorhands*, *Pirates of the Caribbean*, *Finding Neverland*, *Alice in Wonderland*. She even got newsletters from his online fan club. Joss is a member, too.

Netflixing Johnny Depp movies was one thing we could do at my house. She was so mesmerized by him it was like I wasn't even there. Except that one time both Mom and Dad had to leave for a while and asked if I'd watch Ethan. "Sure," Swanee said before I could object. Why did she choose that day to forget about her obsession with Johnny Depp and focus on me?

Her bookcase is filled with trinkets, toys, old dolls. Next to the bookcase are stacks of books. The first time she brought me here, I remember saying, “Did you know you were supposed to put your books *in* the bookcase?”

She gasped. “Seriously?”

Her track trophies are displayed on every available surface—dresser, desk, nightstand, windowsill, floor. One time I tried to count all her trophies. I got to sixty-five before giving up. She has Arvada High Bulldog paraphernalia everywhere—pins and banners and caps. How does someone in her shape just drop dead?

I want to feel her, smell her, see her one last time. I want to taste—

I’m startled by the pinging of her cell. It’s on her bed inside an oversize plastic envelope. I walk over and read the envelope. Hospital issued. Swanee’s clothes and shoes are in it, too. This must’ve been what she was wearing.

Why hasn’t Jewell unpacked the bag? Unless she just couldn’t bear to.

I unzip it and pull out the shirt, lift it to my face. Swanee’s scent is so strong, it steals my breath away. When I close my eyes to inhale her, the phone pings again. I know that ringtone. A text message.

Who would be calling? Surely everyone knows by now. The phone stops before I find it, and I pull out Swan’s sweatpants. They’re folded, like the shirt was. If I unfold everything, will Jewell get mad? I’ll make sure to replace the contents exactly as I found them. The cell pings again and I dig to the bottom of the envelope. It's inside her shoe, so maybe Jewell didn't see or hear it. Maybe a nurse packed Swanee's belongings. Her cell is so distinctive, with its glittery purple cover and bejeweled S W A N on the back. It glows in the dark.

Only Swan would have a glow-in-the-dark phone.

I slide to unlock the cell and see numerous texts and voice mails. I can't answer her voice mails because I don't know her password. I can read her text messages, though. There are 108 unanswered ones. Who in the world…?

The first was sent the day Swanee died, at 5:10 AM.

Buenos dias cariño. Hope you had a good run. Call me when you get home

Who sent this? I was still asleep, still oblivious. Happy. Whole. The caller is LT.

LT. I don't know anyone with those initials.

"What are you doing in here?"

I spin around. "Nothing."

"It doesn't look like nothing," Joss says from the doorway. She's eyeing the bag on the bed, the emptied contents. I hide the cell behind my back.

I say, "I just wanted to…" What? Find Swanee alive?

"Joss." Jewell appears behind her. "Why don't you go entertain your cousins?"

"Those fucking morons?" Joss says.

"Watch your mouth."

"Why? You don't."

Jewell turns her around bodily and swats her butt. Joss gives her mom the finger behind her back.

Jewell says to me, "I can't even bring myself to set foot in here." Her eyes travel around the perimeter. "You don't see any mice or roaches, do you?"

I smile slightly and shake my head. Exhaling the breath I was holding, I say, "I didn't mean to go through her bag."

Jewell stares at the open bag as if it doesn't even register on her reality scale. She blinks and looks up at me. "Does your room look like this?"

"Pretty much," I lie. I'm a slob, too, but Mom forces me to clean once or twice a month.

Jewell points to the window and says, "Would you mind closing that?"

Swanee always liked her window open a crack. She never got cold. Unlike me. I'm always cold.

I see the snow is really coming down. I pull the window shut and lock it. As I'm turning around, Swan's cell pings again and I panic. It's still in my hand. Jewell must not hear, though, because she's leaning against the doorjamb, tears streaming down her face.

I put the phone on vibrate and stick it in my back pocket.

Jewell opens her arms to me and I go to her. "We didn't even get to say good-bye, did we?"

Her tears revive my own.

"Life is so precious," Jewell says in a sob. "So short."

We hold on to each other until the wave recedes. Jewell's smoothing my hair back when I see Mom turn the corner. "Your father and I are ready to go," she says. "If you are."

I want to stay here now. Be close to Swan.

Jewell backs off, wiping her eyes. I ease Swanee's door

shut behind us, but for the life of me, I can't release the handle. Can't let her go.

I say to Mom or Jewell, "Swanee borrowed some things from me."

Jewell asks, "Do you need them today?"

"No. I can come back." I *need* to come back.

"Come tomorrow," Jewell says. "Call first." She walks over to Mom, who's balancing Ethan on her hip, and tenderly touches his chubby cheek with the undersides of her fingers. "Hey there, sweet cakes," she coos.

Ethan whines a little, and then winds up to let loose. "He's tired," Mom says.

Jewell twists her head to meet my eyes over her shoulder. "You're always welcome here, Alix. Don't be a stranger."

Chapter 4

My mother obviously has a sixth sense. I never told her I had a girlfriend, but one morning at breakfast she asked, "When do we get to meet her?"

I felt blazing heat rising up my neck. "Who?"

Mom checked her BlackBerry. "What about Friday night? You could bring her home for dinner."

I muttered, "We're going out."

"Go out after dinner," Dad said. It wasn't a request.

Our relationship was so new and fresh, I didn't want anything to spoil it. What if she didn't like them, or vice versa? Surprisingly, Swanee seemed kind of flattered by the invitation.

She must've smoked a ton of weed before she came, though, because she couldn't stop giggling and her eyes were bloodshot. I could see Mom and Dad exchanging glances.

During dessert, Dad asked, "Where are you two going?"

"Ice-skating," Swanee said.

Really? I thought we were going to a party. Skating sounded much more fun.

On the way out, Dad pulled me aside and handed me his keys. "You drive."

I snagged Swanee's sleeve and told her, "I have to drive."

She covered her mouth and snort-giggled through her fingers. "Busted," she said. "Wha' gave me away?"

Her slurred speech? The bottle of patchouli she'd bathed in?

The next morning I got a text at 6:48 AM:

I picked up my car after my run. Your dad's a total a-hole. Do your parents hate me?

No, of course not, I texted back. My dad has strict rules about DUI or riding with anyone who isn't sober

I was perfectly fine

Except she fell asleep before we even got there. What I didn't add is that is one of Dad's rules I actually agree with.

The next day Mom told me she and Dad wanted to get together with Swanee's parents. "Why?" I asked. Were they going to rat her out?

"Because that's what parents do," Mom said. "They get to know one another."

In what century?

"Oh my God!" Joss shrieked when she heard. "Can I go? I have *got* to see this."

"Can she?" Swanee asked me.

"I don't know why not. Ethan will be there."

"What about Genjko?" Swan asked. "He *is* the family conversationalist." Joss cracked up.

I hoped that meant they weren't serious.

It ended up he didn't come, thank God. I admit I was already more than a little worried about Mom and Dad's reaction to Jewell and Asher. Swanee's parents are free spirits—in an ultracool way. Asher has a long ponytail, and Jewell shows off a lot of skin with her fake-bake tan.

The evening turned out okay. Swanee wasn't high, and neither was Joss. Aside from the bottle of wine that Jewell and Asher put away, everyone was on their best behavior.

The next time I saw Jewell, she asked, "Did we pass inspection?"

My face flared. "With flying colors."

Mom and Dad never talked about the Durbins, even though I had a strong suspicion they didn't approve. And Swanee was careful never to come over again stoned, which I appreciated. If Mom or Dad had forbidden me to see her, it would've been all-out war.

LT's messages go on and on.

6:10 AM: I left you 2 vms. Wassup?

6:15 AM: You were going to text me before you left. Remember?

12:02 PM: Are you having fun? Wish I could've gone with you to Keystone today. Next time

"There won't be a next time," I think out loud. Who is this?

2:12 PM: Call me when you get home. Te amo, mi amore

Swanee was taking Spanish this year as an elective. Personally, I plan to take something fun like photography or screenprinting.

Amore, I repeat to myself. Doesn't that mean *love*?

There were texts throughout last Saturday, into Sunday, and the whole next week. I lie in bed and try to scan them all. A lot are half English, half Spanish.

8:23 AM: Mass this morning then my little bro's b-day party at Chuck E. Cheese's ☺. I probably won't see you this weekend. CALL ME. Te extraño mucho

Monday. 9:03 AM: I'm texting in Am. Hist. Snooze alert. Where are you?

In an urn, I think.

11:45 AM: Call me. Text me. I'm on my way to lunch, but I'll keep my cell on

1:34 PM: Why haven't you called? Are you OK?

"No," I say. "She's not okay."

2:10 PM: Practice. But I'll be done by 3. CALL ME. I left you 100 vms

An exaggeration. Still, I wish I could listen and see who this person is.

3:22 PM: What did I do? Are you mad at me? Please, Swan. Tell me what I did

It'd be a kindness to call this LT person and let her know Swanee will not be returning calls or texts.

I'm startled when my cell rings. It's after midnight.

"Would it be okay if I came over?" Joss asks. "I need to get out of this fucking asylum."

I feel for her, but I can't wallow in her grief, plus mine. I don't think Mom and Dad would be too thrilled about her showing up at this hour, anyway.

"I'm tired," I tell her.

She hesitates a moment, and then disconnects.

Another text comes in from LT:

Please, Swan. Call me. Te amo con todo mi corazón

Whatever that means.

My curiosity gets the best of me. I hit Recent Calls and redial Joss.

"Shouldn't you be asleep?" she says sarcastically.

I deserve that. "Do you know anyone with the initials LT?"

She pauses. "Why do you ask?"

I could tell her I stole—borrowed—Swanee's cell. Or not. "I saw the initials in Swan's room when I was in there."

"Who gave you permission to go in her room, anyway?"

"No one. I was just..." Trespassing? Trying to resurrect her from the dead? Joss was either barred from the room or had more respect than I did.

"Who's LT?" I ask again.

"Where did you see the initials?"

Where? "On a piece of paper."

There's such a long pause, I think Joss has left me hanging.

"Joss?"

"You don't want to know who she is," she says.

"Why?" I ask.

She disconnects again. God, she can be so irritating. On Swanee's cell, I open her contacts list. Great. Her entire list is initials only. AVP. That's me. Alix Van Pelt.

AD. Asher?

GD. Genjko?

JD. Joss or Jewell? Must be Jewell, because Joss got her phone taken away for sending lewd photos to some guy.

LT. She's in here.

RC. Rachel?

Swan doesn't have a very long list. Five or six more contacts.

Another text comes in. Why does she keep calling? Surely she knows Swanee is no longer available to take calls. Her death has been in the newspaper and on TV. How could anyone be so out of touch?

I suppose there could be a simple explanation. LT was out of town. She doesn't read the newspaper. She doesn't live in Colorado—except she mentioned Keystone.

I read the latest text.

Please. Please tell me what I did. Please, Swan. Te amo con todo mi corazón

I get up and grab my laptop off my desk, turn it on. I Google the Spanish phrase.

My breath catches in my throat: *I love you with all my heart.*

Even though it's the middle of night, I'm wide awake. For some unknown, ungodly reason, I reply to her text:

Hey

Immediately, I get a response.

OMG. OMG. OMG. Where have you been?

I reply:

Here. I've been right here

She goes on:

Why didn't you answer? Why didn't you call?

I reply:

I lost my cell

For a week? Why didn't you use cell tracker?

I smack my forehead. Stupid answer.

My iPad's on the fritz ☹

OK. Sorry. Hope you get it working

That sounds like she doesn't believe me. I wouldn't believe me, either.

She texts:

When can we meet? I have a game every night this week, but what about Saturday?

What kind of game? I wonder. What kind of game is she playing? *Te amo.* I'm so sure.

I text her:

We'll talk tomorrow

"Shit," I think aloud. That was a dumb thing to say. Now what?

She texts:

You sure you're OK? You sound mad

I'm not mad

I don't text: I'm dead.

Tomorrow we will talk and I'll get to the bottom of who this LT person is. I'll tell her about Swanee and be done with it.

She texts:

Duerma con los angelitos, querida

I Google the translation: *Sleep with the angels, sweetheart.*

Chapter 5

Swan's phone dings at 7:10 AM:

> Buenos dias, amore. How was your run? We're off to Mass, but I'll get away later so we can talk. Maybe meet? I miss you so much

I don't text back. And I don't call. Last night I turned off Location Services so no one can track Swanee's cell using her GPS. I notice Swan's battery is nearly drained, and I know the best thing to do would be to just let the cell die. Burn it and bury it with Swanee.

I page through her texts to find the last one I sent her.

Friday. The day before.

> What time do you want me there in the morning?

For snowboarding at Keystone. Which we never did. Keystone. How would LT know about Keystone? I feel so confused and sad and empty, all at once. I plug in to my nano to let my music drown out the grief. Unfortunately, most of the songs on my playlist are the ones Swanee loaded, and that only intensifies the pain. Removing the earbuds, I cover my head with my pillow. I must fall asleep because the sound of my name jolts me back to consciousness.

The door opens wider.

"Alix? It's almost noon," Mom says.

So what? Time is irrelevant.

"Jewell's on the phone. She wants to know what time you're coming over to get your things."

It takes me a moment to clear my head. I scramble out of bed and realize I'm wearing the same clothes I wore to Swanee's service.

Mom's disappeared.

Downstairs, Dad's at the table reading the paper, while Ethan is making a gaggy mess of his breakfast. Mom motions me to the cordless, which she set on the breakfast bar.

I grab it and head into the living room. "Hi." I clear my throat.

"Alix, we decided last night to go to Hawaii. We've been saving up for a vacation, and now is as good a time as any. We need to get out of here and, you know, regroup. We're leaving in a few hours, so if you want your things, could you come over and get them?"

"Yeah, of course." I want to ask if I can go with them. To... regroup. "I just need to get dressed." Rather, changed. "I'll be there in fifteen minutes."

A duffel nearly clobbers me as it's tossed down the hall, but Asher yanks me out of the way. "Watch it, Genjko." Then he says to me, "Sorry about that."

Genjko's anger is palpable. He rarely leaves his room, so I'm sure he's being coerced to go on this trip.

"Take whatever's yours and I'll donate the rest to Goodwill," Jewell says to me.

"No!" Joss cries, dumping her backpack on the pile of luggage. "Everything she has belongs to me."

Jewell says coolly to Joss, "What makes you think that?"

"She was my sister." Joss's voice trembles.

"We don't need bad karma in this house," Jewell replies. "Right, Genjko?"

He storms out the door. I wonder how he feels about Swanee's death. Or about anything at all.

Joss pushes past me and slams out after him.

"There's a set of keys under the ceramic frog on the front porch," Jewell tells me. "Just lock up on your way out."

I stand and watch until they drive away. The heater cranks off with a hiss, jarring me out of my stupor.

My footsteps creak as I walk down the hallway. Swanee's door is closed, the same way I left it. I brought an empty backpack, and as I begin to slog through the flotsam and jetsam of Swanee's life, I notice there's more of me here than I thought. Swan borrowed a pair of sweats and jeans and two long-sleeved thermal shirts. A lot of the button jewelry I made her is strewn haphazardly across the floor, along with library books that will eventually be overdue.

My knees go weak and I have to sit. Then lie down. I bundle a blue sweatshirt under my head and curl into a ball. "Why did you have to die?" I whisper.

Silence presses against my body and a tear rolls out of the corner of my eye.

"I need you. I love you."

My cell jingles in my bag. The ringtone for Mom. I let it go to voice mail and stay still until I begin to shiver from the cold of the floor, or the lack of human warmth. I retrieve my phone and listen to Mom's message:

"Are you almost done? I need you to do some grocery shopping for me."

Chores, chores, chores. Swanee never had any chores or responsibilities.

Mom adds at the end, "I'll leave the list on the fridge."

Lists, lists, lists. I'd been living under a fascist regime until I met Swanee and saw the light of liberation.

I want to memorize every square inch of this room. My cell is in my hand, so I snap pictures.

I have dozens of pictures of Swanee on my cell. Goofy shots of her making faces, sticking out her tongue or crossing her eyes; candid shots of her in the moment. A close-up of us kissing.

I need to stop torturing myself, but I can't let her cell die. Her charger is plugged into the wall, so I pull it out and drop it into my bag. On my way to the door, my foot crunches a CD. I bend over to pick it up. There's no label. Only a line written in permanent marker:

♥ LIANA

Before I even make it home, Swan's cell pings. I swerve to the curb and read it while I'm idling.

> Hi. You didn't call me. I left you a vm. Did you get it? I can probably get away to meet you later today. If you want. Call me. Por favor!

I text back:

Where do you want to meet and when?

She texts:

Our regular place? Like, 4:30?

Shit. What's their regular place?

I text:

Let's go to a new place. I have something to tell you

There's a long pause before her next text arrives.

Is it good or bad?

When I don't respond right away, she texts:

If it's bad, I don't want to come

She has to. She needs to know.

She texts again:

Good or bad, I don't care. I miss you. Let's meet at Twin Peaks

What's Twin Peaks? Dad would never let me drive in the mountains by myself. Screw that. I need to meet her. I text:

OK

She texts:

In front of the theater. 4:30?

Fine, I text.

Te amo

I don't even know what to say to that. I text:

See you

Suddenly, it hits me. Facebook. I'll find her there. At least now I know her first name, assuming LT is Liana from the CD.

Dad practically assaults me as I'm coming through the garage door. "What took so long?" he asks.

Hello to you, too.

He shoves the grocery list at me, along with a fistful of cash, and then heads for the stairs. I can see why he's in a hurry, and a mood. Ethan has icky diarrhea that's running out the side of his diaper and down Dad's arm. "Thanks for helping out," he says.

If he's being sarcastic, I can't tell.

I think illegible handwriting must be a course in medical school, because Mom's scrawl is impossible to decipher. I finally figure out that "park chips" is pork chops. Is "bd" bread or baby diapers? I'll buy both.

By the time I get home from Safeway, the house is quiet. Dad's in his office working and Ethan must be napping. Dad left me a note on the kitchen table:

If you could start the laundry, I'll buy you a Mercedes.

His idea of a joke. I don't know how many times I've asked for a car so we wouldn't have to share. He always has the same excuses: more car payments, exorbitant insurance costs, we don't need three cars, blah, blah.

Swanee told me she got her Smart car the day she turned sixteen. She even got to design it herself, online. Coolest car in the world.

Downstairs in the laundry room, there's a mountain of clothes to be sorted and washed. If Mom and Dad expect me to do them all, I'll be here for a week. I stuff as many clothes as possible in one load and pour in a cup of detergent.

Then I sprint upstairs and grab my laptop. Propped against the headboard, I log in and link to Facebook. I can't get into Swan's home page, but I can see that dozens and dozens of people have left messages on her profile wall:

RIP, Swan.

You'll be missed.

RIP. RIP. RIP.

My eyes pool with tears and I want to send her an iheart, the way I do—did—every day.

She only has fifty-two friends. She was picky about who she'd add. In the Search area under her friends list, I enter *Liana T.* Nobody comes up. Maybe I'm wrong about the first name. I enter *L* and three people pop up. Lyndi Tartakoff. Don't know her. I link to her profile and see she's from Michigan. I'm curious how Swanee knows her, but she can't be the LT I'm looking for if she wants to meet Swanee in their regular place. Libby Tyndal-Weir. She was in my keyboarding class in eighth grade. Lili Thompson. I click on her profile and see she's Swanee's aunt. I think I saw her at the memorial service.

Dead end.

Next I Google *Twin Peaks.*

There are a bunch of businesses in Colorado beginning with *Twin Peaks*, and also a mall. If we're meeting at a theater, she must mean the Twin Peaks Mall. It's in Longmont, about forty minutes away. I print directions and check the time: 3:45. I'm going to have to book it.

How often did they meet at their "regular spot"? What did they do there? My imagination is running wild, and I wish Swanee were here so I could ask about LT. I'm sure there's a rational explanation for a girl calling Swan a hundred times a day and telling her, "I love you. Sleep with the angels." It's almost as if she knew that's where Swanee was headed.

* * *

"I'm going out for a while," I tell Dad.

He says automatically, "Out where?"

Why do I have to justify everything I do? Swanee hated that my parents treat me like a child. She thought it was "belittling."

"Just out," I reply.

He swivels in his desk chair and meets my eyes.

"I got the shopping done and the laundry started. I promise to finish it when I get back."

For a minute I think he's going to say no and I'll have to sneak off with the car. Which I've never done.

But his face softens and he goes, "Be careful."

Shock. My brain continues his thought: Because if you total the car, we're both out wheels. Then I feel guilty for even going there.

Traffic is heavy for a Sunday, as if everyone got out of church at the same time. I'm the one praying while cars zip in and out of lanes, honking or shooting the gaps. I know I drive too slowly on the highway, but going seventy-five makes me feel like the Prius is swerving out of control. Or I am.

Even with the directions, I get lost between Boulder and Longmont and it takes me more than an hour to get to Twin Peaks. I race to the theater entrance. When I check my watch it's 5:10. Shit. I'm never late.

Swanee is. Was. She was always late, so maybe LT won't have left yet.

A movie must have just ended because people are swarming out of the lobby. There's a line at the ticket window, and people are waiting to buy refreshments. How will I ever find her?

I scan the crowd, searching for a clue. She's a girl. Duh. Is she around my age? She sends texts in Spanish, so is she Hispanic? That eliminates maybe a quarter of the people here. This is impossible. I should've made a sign to hold up: LT, ARE YOU LOOKING FOR SWANEE DURBIN?

Hold on. How dumb. Maybe there's a picture of her on Swanee's cell. I dig it out of my bag and scroll through her pages and pages of pics. One in particular catches my eye. It's Joss exposing her breasts. Yikes! I should probably delete it, but Swanee must've had a reason for keeping it on there.

The only other pictures left on her phone are of herself and Joss, acting silly, in crazy outfits. There isn't even one of me. That isn't right. I know she took dozens of pictures of us together. Why would she have deleted them all?

Swanee said I was the most beautiful person she knew, but maybe she meant on the inside.

I stand across from the theater against the mirrored wall until the crowd thins. Until there's only a handful of people. Two girls are sitting on a bench acting as if they're waiting for someone. They look like they might be in high school. I approach, clearing my throat.

"Um, Liana?" I say to the closest one. "LT?"

They halt their conversation midsentence and gawk at me. No, they're too young. More like middle schoolers, just wearing dark, heavy makeup. LT could be younger, I think.

The two get up and head off down the mall, talking and giggling.

I check out every passerby. She wouldn't be passing by. She'd be waiting.

A dark-haired girl in a short skirt and layered tops is standing just inside the lobby, by the video games. The hairs on the back of my neck tingle. That's her. I know it.

I take two steps toward her, and then stop. A sudden bout of shyness paralyzes me. I can't do this.

The girl, LT, texts on her cell and Swan's phone pings in my bag.

There's a Piercing Pagoda a few yards down the mall, so I duck around the cart to read her message.

Where are you? I've been waiting over an hour

How long will she wait for Swanee? I wonder. Until she knows the truth, she'll be waiting the rest of her life.

Why didn't I have Joss call and convey the news to Liana before she left for Hawaii to "regroup"? She obviously knows her. Or is she just jerking me around? I can't do it. I hurry down the mall, through the food court, and out the exit. All the way home, I hear Swan's cell pinging. At a McDonald's, I stop to use the restroom. While I'm in the stall, I read her messages.

Where were you? I waited an hour and a half. Why are you doing this to me?

I stare at the message for a long time, and then text:

Sorry. Ran out of gas

She texts back:

You might've called and told me that!

Good. She's mad. Maybe now she'll stop calling and this nightmare will be over.

At home I find the CD from Swanee's room sitting on my player and slide it in. The first song makes my head spin.

"Livin' la Vida Loca."

"Alix?" Mom opens my door. "Dinner's ready. And by the way, thanks for doing the laundry."

She leaves. That was definitely sarcasm.

I slide into my seat at the table and say, "I'm sorry. I started the laundry, and then forgot."

"Where did you go for three hours?" Dad asks.

"It wasn't that long." Was it? I think fast. "To church. I thought praying might help."

That shuts Mom and Dad up. Wow. If lying is an SAT category, I'm going to ace it. We eat in silence, except for Ethan smacking his lips and slapping his high-chair tray.

I hear every tick of the clock and wish I had the magical power to turn back time. I might've persuaded Swanee to forget her run just this once so we could leave earlier; asked if Jewell and Asher would stop in Idaho Springs for breakfast on our way up to Keystone to hit the slopes; somehow convinced her that snowboarding would be plenty of exercise for one day.

Mom interrupts my thoughts. "You haven't eaten anything."

I look down at my plate and feel nauseated. "I'm not hungry. If you'll excuse me—"

"You're not leaving the table until you eat something." Mom spoons another glop of rice cereal into Ethan's mouth.

I don't even remember putting food on my plate. Mom must've doled it out when I wasn't looking. Except the peas and mashed potatoes are mixed together, and only I do that.

"Eat," she orders me.

I do as she says because I'm always the obedient daughter. Swanee never understood why I didn't just tell them to cram it. I could never explain.

Ethan whimpers, spits out his food, and then lets out a screech that hurts my ears so badly that I plug them. Mom presses the backs of her fingers against his forehead and says, "He feels warm. With that diarrhea, I wonder if he has an intestinal bug, or the flu. Maybe he never really got over his pertussis. I need to take his temperature." She lifts him out of his high chair to take him into the living room. I get up with her, but her hand pushes down on my shoulder. "Eat," she says.

I shovel a forkful of potato into my mouth at the same time Ethan projectile vomits his curdled dinner all over the table and down my front.

Forcing down a dry heave, I push back my chair and say, "I'm out of here."

Dad gets up to wet a washcloth for Mom.

Upstairs in my bathroom, I strip and take a long shower. Nothing like the odor and texture of baby puke to stimulate the senses. Shuddering, I log on and link to Facebook, and then click on Swanee's profile. Her picture is a rainbow equality symbol. It's comforting to see that she says she's in a relationship with me. I read through the profile I know so well. Activities: running track, snowboarding, being with friends, partying. Interests: texting, chatting, not shaving my legs ha ha, indie music, hard rock, medium rock, rock candy, candy apples, candy corn. She supports all the same animal rights and human rights organizations I do: HRC,

GSA, Rainbow Alley, the Trevor Project. Everything about her screams GAY.

Mom opens the door. "Your brother has a pretty high temp, so your dad and I are going to run him over to the hospital."

"Okay."

She sets a new plate of food on my desk. "Eat," she says.

Like I ever will again now.

"It's probably just a virus. But I want him checked out. Would you mind terribly cleaning up the kitchen?"

Yes, I would mind terribly.

When I don't answer, she goes, "Or I'll do it when we get home."

She knows the room will be spotless when she returns.

"I'll call you if it's serious or we're going to be late getting back. Eat."

"I will," I snap.

She gives me a steely look before closing the door. I feel sort of bad for raising my voice.

But why? It should be my choice whether I eat or not.

Swan's cell is silent, and so is mine. Tears well in my eyes, but I don't want to cry. It won't bring Swanee back. I clomp downstairs and load the dishwasher, glad for something to do, even if it only takes five minutes. Thankfully, someone swabbed up Ethan's mess. Swan and I used to talk about finding a small studio apartment in Arizona, rather than living in the dorm. A place we could paint, furnish, decorate. Call our own.

Now I'm afraid I'll always be alone.

I need to go, get out of here. Take a drive. Get as far away as possible from silence and death and the thought of what might have been.

Chapter 6

If I'm distancing myself from silence and death, why do I drive to Crown Hill Cemetery and park at the mausoleum? A few weeks ago Swanee and I came here to see what was inside. From a distance, it looked like a white marble castle rising from the cemetery grounds, and she was sure it was filled with ghosts.

"My life's passion is to be a ghost hunter," she said with a twinkle in her eye. "Bet you didn't know that."

At the time, I laughed. But the mausoleum had always creeped me out, and I told her I didn't want to go in.

"Because you're scared of ghosts?"

"Because it seems, I don't know, irreverent."

"When did you get all religious?"

"I didn't. It's just…" I gazed at the cold marble building full of bodies and shivered. I *so* didn't want to go in.

"Oh, come on," Swan said. She opened the door, and what could I do but follow her?

The mausoleum was six floors of deceased people, their caskets stored inside the walls with their names engraved on plaques outside. Some had flowerpots with bouquets in them. Since a lot of the flowers were fresh, I assumed they were renewed frequently. Swan remarked on it: "You wouldn't want dead people to have dead flowers." Her voice echoed eerily.

I remember the stale air and the sense that the walls were closing in on us as we wandered down each hall. And we had to explore every floor. Read every name on every plaque.

"Swan," I whispered more than once. "Let's go."

"It's crazy," she said. "People spending money on this shit."

I felt claustrophobic and dizzy, so I plopped down on a bench and dropped my head between my knees to stop the vertigo. When I could focus again, I lifted my head and saw a small plaque across from me. I got up to read it, ran my fingers across the lettering. Swan returned and stood beside me.

"This one was only a baby," I told her. The birth and death dates were five days apart. My mother might have cared for this baby in the neonatal care unit. She might've been there when he died.

Swan said, "You're not going to cry, are you?"

I actually thought I might. "Can we please go now?"

Bumping my shoulder, she said, "Exorcise your inner wuss."

I curled a lip at her, but she was right.

Now I get out of the car and head toward the mausoleum entrance, but stop just short. I can't go in. Too much death. Too many ghosts.

Instead, I walk around Crown Hill, noting how the headstones get smaller and smaller the farther out I go, as if the people who died more recently are less important. A guy in a golf cart drives up to me on the path and says, "We'll be closing in fifteen minutes."

I didn't know graveyards closed. "Okay," I tell him. I guess you're only supposed to honor your loved ones between certain hours of the day.

I send Swanee a mental message as I head back to the car: You'll never die in my head or heart.

The next morning, Monday, I ask the librarian if I can eat my lunch in the media center. She gives me the pity look that everyone else has been casting me all morning. "Yes," she says. "But only for today. Okay?"

Today is all I need. It's twelve thirty here, eight thirty in Hawaii.

I call Joss. This morning she texted me, telling me to call her ASAP and giving me a number. I don't know where she got the phone, but I am glad she has one because I need to ask her some questions. She picks up on the fourth ring, sounding groggy.

"Hi," I say. "It's Alix."

"I need you to get me some stuff from Swan's room," she says.

"Are you having fun?" I ask. Stupid question. I almost

ask if she's regrouped, but that'd be two stupid questions in a row.

"I want my wigs and makeup kit. I have a bunch of clothes in there, but I don't care about them. I definitely want Swan's cell. I know she had it on her when she... Look in that hospital bag."

I'm barely listening. "Tell me about Liana."

She doesn't say anything.

"I know her first name, Joss. What's her last name?"

Joss yawns. "Why do you want to know?"

"I just do."

There's another long pause. "It's your stake through the heart."

My what? She's so melodramatic.

"It's Torres."

Torres. LT has a name. Liana Torres. It makes her more real.

"Who is she to Swanee?" I ask.

Joss says, "You don't have to worry. She won't find out about you."

What does that mean? Can't she answer one question without talking around it?

Now I'm more confused than ever. "Who is she to Swanee?" I ask again.

"Don't you mean *was*?"

I'm still having a hard time thinking of Swan in the past tense.

Joss says, "If Swan wanted you to know, she would've told you."

I want to throttle her. "Maybe she was going to tell me, but she didn't get a chance." Did Joss ever think of that? Because I have—about a hundred times.

Joss doesn't take the bait.

"Please, Joss. I need to know."

"Why?"

Because we didn't have that much time together, and there are so many things that were left unsaid, and undone. I answer quietly, "Just because."

Joss sighs, sounding exactly like Swanee. "Liana was her girlfriend."

My jaw unhinges. I say, "But I am—was—"

"Her ex. She broke up with her after she met you."

Relief washes over me.

"Get Swan's iPad for me, too. She has a lot of pictures of us on it. Just put everything under my bed so Jewell won't see it."

I'm still processing this conversation. Something isn't adding up, like the time line. And Liana's ongoing texts. "When did they break up, exactly?"

"I don't know the date and time. Exactly."

"But they did break up."

"I told you they did. Are you calling me a liar?"

"No." I take a deep breath. "How can you be so sure Liana doesn't know about me?" I ask Joss. I know about her.

Joss says, "Because Swan gave her a fake last name. Liana didn't know anything about Swanee's real life."

Oh my God. That explains the texts. "Is there a possibility she doesn't know Swanee's dead?"

Joss goes, "Fuck."

"What name did Swanee give her?"

"Swanelle Delaney. I came up with it."

Like that's important? "Do you know her? Personally?"

"I met her a few times. At the games Swanee took me to. She's a bitch."

Again with the games. "What games? Where?"

"She's a cheerleader at Greeley West."

What about cheers being stuck-up sluts? Maybe that only applied to Betheny. "How long were they together?"

"You're really a masochist, aren't you?"

"I just think someone should tell her about Swanee. If, um, she doesn't already know."

"When you find her phone, look in Swan's contacts list. She might still have the number. Text her. Anonymously, of course."

I almost slip and say I know Liana's number. "Don't you think she should be told in person?"

"By who? Me? No way."

Well, I'm not going to call or text her. That'd be the cruelest way ever to deliver heartbreaking news about someone you're obviously still in love with.

I hear voices in the background and Joss says, "We're off to score some native weed. Want me to bring you back some?"

"No. Do you know when you'll be home?"

She disconnects without answering the question.

One piece of the puzzle is in place. If Liana didn't know

Swanee's last name, it's conceivable she hasn't connected the dots of Swanee's death.

And now, with Joss out of town, it's my sole responsibility to tell Liana. In fact, I have a burning desire to know everything about her because I think she's the key to cracking a safe full of secrets about Swanee.

Chapter 7

Greeley is a cow town north of Arvada. I Google Greeley West to check out the sports schedule and note that the only home event this week is wrestling on Thursday. That morning I ask Dad if I can borrow the car and he says, "A blizzard is rolling in later."

I figure I can get to Greeley and back in an hour, hour and a half. Telling Liana won't take long, depending on the number of questions she hits me with.

Dad says, "You sure you don't want me to take you and pick you up?"

The way he has ever since I was in elementary school and the weather was bad. I click my tongue in disgust. "I think I can drive six blocks in the snow."

Dad sets a stack of pancakes in front of me and says, "You can walk six blocks, too."

"Or I could drive." I feel angry at him and I don't know why. I'm angry at the world. "Please? I swear I'll be careful."

Dad cradles Ethan on his lap with a bottle while he squirts syrup on his pancakes. "It's not that I don't trust you, Alix. I know you're a good driver."

So what's the problem? "Can I take it?"

He cuts into his pancakes and says, "All right. But if it gets really bad and you don't feel comfortable driving home, call me."

"And you'll do what?"

He chews and swallows. "Bundle up Bubba here, and hoof it up the hill to rescue you." He smiles.

He would, too. Why does he have to be so irritatingly... Dad?

Around noon the snow starts with a fury. Dad calls me at lunch and asks, "Are they letting you out early?"

"Not that I know of," I tell him.

"I really don't want you driving—"

"Dad, it's six blocks. I'll be fine. If nothing else, I'll just put it in neutral and slide down the hill."

He doesn't laugh.

I skip Physics class and race to the Prius, slipping and sliding through the parking lot. The sheet of ice tests the law that a body in motion stays in motion until it butt-checks the ground. Wadsworth Boulevard is a skating rink, as they say, but I take it slow, eventually exiting I-70 onto I-76, heading for Greeley.

Dad would literally kill me if he knew.

People are driving around thirty on the highway, and even that seems too fast. When I finally reach the Greeley city limits, my jaw aches from clenching it so hard.

The snow's heavier here, and visibility is almost zero. The map I printed out to the school reads, "Exit west toward Loveland, approx. two miles."

I check the dashboard clock: 3:49. The match starts at four.

Greeley West is easy to spot, with its sign reading SPARTAN PRIDE. The building is a one-story brick, newer than Arvada. I take a left past the school to the west parking lot. It's full, so I have to park a block away.

The snow and wind buffet me across the street, to the wide front steps, and through the door.

Inside I hear the band and see groups of people on their way to the gym. My cell reads 3:53, and I want to make sure I catch Liana before the match starts. I realize this is not the ideal time to tell her that her ex is dead, because either she'll have to pretend nothing's wrong or she'll lose it completely and have to leave. I don't really know her, so I have no idea how she'll react.

Suddenly a girl appears out of the restroom. A cheerleader. I recognize her from the theater. Our eyes meet and she says, "Hi," and then turns to go.

"Liana." A lump forms in my throat and I swallow it down. She swivels back. "I'm Alix. A, um, friend of Swanee's."

She has these caramel-colored eyes, enormous, the size of half dollars. "Who's Swanee?"

Shit. She didn't even know her real name. "Swanelle?"

"Oh. Swan. She never mentioned a friend named Alex." A buzzer blares from the gym and Liana adds, "I have to go."

"I'm Swan's..." I want to say "girlfriend," but something holds me back. "I need to tell you something."

She looks toward the gym, and then back to me. Her expression is expectant.

How to do this?

I say, really fast, "She died. She was running and she had a heart attack. A cardiac arrest." I don't really know the difference. I hope she doesn't ask.

All I can do is stare at this girl while she stares at me.

Liana starts shaking her head. I feel her disbelief. Not horror or grief. That'll come later.

I tell her, "She died on February second. That Saturday morning."

Liana's eyes slit. "You're lying. Swan's alive. I talked to her yesterday."

You texted her, I want to say. You never actually talked. "Check the news reports."

"I read about that girl who died. But there were no pictures, and her name was different. At the time I thought it was strange for two people to have such unusual first names. The last name was different, too, though, and she went to a different school."

I can imagine Jewell and Asher not wanting Swanee's picture splashed all over the news and in the paper. What school did Swanee tell Liana she attended? I wonder. "She gave you false information," I say. "Her real name is—was—Swanee Durbin. And she went to Arvada."

Liana's eyes bore into mine. "So who's been texting me?"

I open my mouth to tell her the truth, but what comes out is, "Someone's been texting you?"

"Joss," she hisses.

"No. She wouldn't." She couldn't because I have the phone.

"Is this one of Swan's pranks? Because it's not funny. It's cruel and evil. And so are you and Joss for going along with it." Liana whirls and sprints off, disappearing into the gym.

Oh, God. I slump against the wall, closing my eyes. I should be proud that I found the courage to tell her, but all I feel is sick to my stomach.

I have to drive all the way home riding the brakes and skidding into snowbanks to keep from hitting the car in front at me. Dad'll need to have the brake pads replaced and the tires realigned, or whatever. It's almost dark by the time I pull into the driveway. Mom and Dad are both in the kitchen, looking pissed. "Where have you been?" Dad asks. "We've been calling you for the last four hours."

Four hours? I check the microwave clock and see that he's right. It's almost eight.

I'm not about to tell him I've been in Greeley.

Mom seethes. "I even called the Durbins."

That gives me an out. "Sorry, I didn't hear their phone ring. And my cell was on vibrate."

"Alix, I told you they need time to themselves."

"They're not home. They went to Hawaii."

Mom and Dad exchange a frown.

"To regroup," I add. "I told Jewell I'd water her plants while they were gone." Where did that lie come from? "Plus, it's quiet over there, so I can study."

Up in his room, as if on cue, Ethan begins to cry. Dad heads for the stairs.

"Did you even once think to call us, that we might be worried about you?" Mom says.

I did think to call, but then other priorities intervened. "I said I was sorry."

She gives me her classic "you're the most irresponsible person on the face of the planet" look. Then adds, "We ate without you."

Like it's the worst punishment in the world to miss our family meal.

I look up Liana Torres on Facebook. Naturally, her profile is set to private. All I can see is her recent activity, which is a change in her profile picture. She's gorgeous. A pang of jealousy shoots through me and I can understand why Swanee would want me to break off my relationship with Betheny, even if it was only friendship.

If I want to learn more about Swanee through Liana, the only way is for her to accept a friend request from me so I can check out her albums and read her wall and time line. She might initially add me, until she figures out I'm that lying bitch who showed up at her school to tell her the truth about Swanee. I could fake a name, like Swanee did. Or use Alixandra. Or remove Swanee Durbin as my girlfriend.

Forget it. That will remain permanent on my Facebook.

Thinking about the hatred in Liana's eyes when she thought Joss was playing a joke on her brings tears to my eyes. Why did I lead her on, let her believe Swanee was still alive? Why didn't I just call after the first text and let her know what happened on Swanee's run?

It was selfish of me to want to know who Liana was. In time Swanee would've told me, if I'd asked. She didn't like talking about her past. But we didn't keep secrets, either.

I could let it go and allow Liana to believe whatever she wants, if it weren't for the fact that she blames Joss now. I don't know why I care, but I do.

No, it's going to stop here. Liana needs to know the truth. Period.

I send her a friend request and wait to see what'll happen.

Surprisingly, Dad asks if I want a ride to school. He doesn't seem mad about yesterday, but I worry that he'll never let me borrow the car again.

"That's okay," I say. "But thanks."

In the mudroom, I pull on my boots and see that Mom's already left for the hospital. Then it hits me. I return to the kitchen and ask Dad, "How's Ethan? Did they figure out what's wrong?"

Without looking up from his iPad, where he reads the newspaper every morning, he says, "I wondered when you were going to remember him."

My face flares. I remember. I care that he's sick. I just have a lot on my mind.

"It's an intestinal bug that seems to be going around," Dad says. "He probably caught it at day care."

Why doesn't he add, When you didn't want to babysit?

"But he'll be all right?"

Dad meets my eyes and nods. "Will you?"

It takes me a moment to absorb his meaning. So many feelings well up inside, I want to run to him and have him hold me, tell me everything's going to be okay. But we don't have that kind of relationship.

I miss Swan so much.

I can't even respond as I race out of the garage and punch the key code to close the door behind me. Dad's shoveled the driveway, but not all the side streets have been cleared. I trudge up Sixty-Ninth, the hill that leads to Dover Court and Swanee's house.

On the spur of the moment, I decide to ditch. I'd never skipped a whole day of school until I met Swanee. She persuaded me to do a lot of things I'd never done. Like smoke weed. And drink. Begin to liberate myself, the way she had. Apparently, she took off from school whenever she felt like it, and Jewell and Asher didn't care. When I told her my parents would flip, she said what I already knew: "Haven't they heard that slavery was abolished?"

Her house is older than ours. More shabby. We moved farther west, to a newer subdivision, when Mom got her job at St. Anthony. She wanted me to transfer to Arvada West, which scores a higher grade than Arvada, or go to a charter school. But all my friends are at Arvada. Betheny, the GSA, mathletes, ski club. And then I met Swanee.

I know Mom has high expectations of me following in her footsteps and becoming a doctor. I hate to tell her that dealing with death on a daily basis would harden my heart like lava. Or eat me alive from the inside out.

I find the Durbins' key under the frog on the porch and let myself in. Before heading to Swanee's room, I wander around, touching objects, picking up interesting artifacts. Swanee told me Jewell and Asher met while backpacking across Europe. I always thought it'd be cool to take off like that, camp out, meet people on the road. Swan said, "Fuck that shit." She required hot water for showers, real food, and flushing toilets.

My attention is drawn to an object on the mantel. The urn. I take it down and open the lid. The ashes aren't loose inside; they're stored in a plastic bag. They aren't black, the way I imagined. They're gray. I never viewed Swanee as a gray person. She was every color of the rainbow.

I replace the urn on the mantel and go down the hall to Swanee's room.

It's exactly the same. I don't know why I expected it to be different.

My vision blurs and I peer up at the ceiling. "Can you see me, Swan?" I struggle for words. "Can you feel me?"

No answer. A tear trickles down one cheek and I wipe it away angrily. Kicking through her mess, I stop at the bed and stare at the hospital bag. Untouched except by me. I whirl and slide down the side of the mattress to the floor, covering my head with my arms. "Please, God," I murmur. "If you can really perform miracles, bring her back to me. I can't live without her."

Swan's cell pings, startling me. I dig it out of my bag.

Stupid. I don't believe in psychic communication, but maybe...

It's Liana.

This chick came to my school and told me you were dead. But I guess you know that. Not funny, Swan

It's the truth.

CALL ME

Why can't she get it through her thick head that Swanee is gone, that the person who died *was* her Swanee, not Swanelle Delaney, or whatever stupid name she used?

Because of me, my deception. I should take her up on her offer, call and tell her the whole truth, including my part in leading her on by texting. I press her number, but after one ring I chicken out. It's all so... wrong.

Swanee's cell rings in my hand. I can't answer it. The ringing stops and after a minute the blip for a voice mail sounds. No doubt it's her leaving a string of Spanish swear words.

I rummage around for all the items Joss wants. Her room is to the right of Swanee's. It's a pit, too. I shove everything I retrieved for her under the bed, including Swanee's cell. But when I get to the door, I turn around, go back, and snatch up the cell.

It's mine. Aside from the few memories I'll always have, Swanee's cell is my only connection to her, and I'm not ready to cut the cord. I'll never be ready.

Back in Swan's room, I go through everything to make sure I'm not leaving anything behind. I'm not coming back here; it's too painful. On her dresser, under a pile of clothes, there's a silver necklace with a cross. A religious symbol? She never wore much jewelry, including all the earrings I made for her. I'd never make her a cross. It's obvious who gave her that.

I sweep through Swan's closet. Her clothes, the ones on hangers, are all familiar. I bury my face in her pink-and-blue ski sweater, the one she wore the day we met.

I wonder if Jewell will miss it. Fuck. I'm taking the sweater.

I rifle maniacally through every drawer, tossing shirts and shorts and underwear to the floor. Spinning around, I see her bookcase, her stack of books beside it. I examine every book. Is it mine, hers, the library's? I throw them one after another against the wall.

I feel wild, out of control. It's so unfair. I'm mad at everyone, the universe. Most of all I'm mad at Swanee for dying and taking from me the most precious thing I ever owned. I didn't own her, but she was mine. Mine, Liana. Do you hear me?

"Swanee, you had no right!" I know it doesn't make sense to blame her, because it's not like she meant to die. "But you did it. And you left me here, alone, to pick up the pieces." An uncontrollable rage burbles up inside me.

There are magazines on her nightstand and I toss them off. A black-and-white essay book, or journal, goes flying. I haven't seen it before. I flip through the pages, noting the handwriting isn't Swanee's.

On the first page it reads:

I love you forever.
Para siempre, mi amore.

L.

My breathing comes in rasps and I feel like I'm having a heart attack. Forever was us, Swanee and me. Liana was out of the picture.

I rip the first few pages out and kick them under the bed.

Bending over, I catch my breath. Calm myself. Time passes in waves. Surveying the mess I made, I think, Jewell will be livid that I ransacked Swanee's room. Carefully, lovingly, I put things back where I found them, best as I can remember.

Mom's there when I get home. She pushes up from the sofa. "The school called."

Shit. "I didn't feel well."

"So where were you all day? And don't tell me the Durbins'."

I won't tell her anything, then. I run up the stairs and shut my door. A few seconds later, Mom opens it. She could knock, at least. She comes in my room and sits on my bed. I roll away from her, wishing that she'd just leave. That everyone would just leave me alone.

"I understand how hard this is for you, honey," she says. "You need closure. Maybe you should talk to a grief counselor."

"I'm fine," I mutter.

"You're not fine. You're hurting, and you're bottling up your feelings. Taking out your anger on everyone around you won't do anyone any good."

That's so deep, Mom, I think. You should've gone into psychiatry.

When I don't respond, she exhales heavily. Then she gets up and goes.

Closure. I almost laugh. There is no closure. No such thing. Only open wounds. I can't even imagine they'll heal to the point of scabbing over.

Chapter 8

As I'm reading all the new condolence messages people have left on my Facebook wall, I see that my friend request to Liana was accepted. It feels bizarre that she'd confirm me after her text to Swanee yesterday.

I link to her profile. She has 488 friends. It doesn't necessarily mean she's popular. She's accepting friends at will, the way I do. Not that I have people waiting in line. I search for Swanee's name in Liana's friends, but it's not there. "Swanelle Delaney" is. Liana's in a relationship with a person who doesn't exist.

But then, so am I.

Liana has lots of photo albums. The first is a series of her in her cheerleading uniform, doing split jumps and contorting her body in midair. There's a shot of a squad of cheerleaders performing leg kicks in a line, then one of them lifting her onto a pyramid. Next, she's on top, raising a pom-pom.

The next album is Liana with a litter of kittens around

her. She's holding one up, nose to nose. A little calico. The expression on Liana's face is so serene. If Mom weren't allergic, I'd have a houseful of cats.

A family album includes photos of people at Christmas. There's a photo of Liana in flannel pajamas, sitting with a baby on her lap and opened packages all around. The baby has her dark hair and huge eyes. Is it hers? Is that why Swanee thought cheerleaders were sluts? Liana's relatives, I assume, are hamming it up for the camera, and then the family is sitting around a dining room table with a turkey and all the trimmings.

There's a wedding where Liana is one of the bridesmaids.

Then I see an album titled SWAN.

The pictures go on for pages and pages. The Smart car, Liana hanging out the window, waving to someone. Liana and Swanee wearing Joss's wigs at a roller rink. I bet Joss was elated about that—if she even knew. How often did Liana go to Swanee's house, or stay over?

I don't care I don't care I don't care.

Another picture with Swanee pinning Liana's arms to the ground. The two of them laughing, gazing into each other's eyes. Kissing.

I know I wasn't Swanee's first, but it's hard to look at the evidence of her loving someone else.

How long were they together? I wonder. Because I have maybe ten pictures in my Facebook albums. She was always telling me, "Don't post my picture. I look fat."

Which was ridiculous. She was a lean, mean, running machine.

Joss would know how long Swan and Liana were together. In fact, she might be the one who took all the pictures of Swanee and Liana.

I call Joss that night and the first thing she says is, "Did you get my stuff?"

"Yeah. It's in your room. I didn't find her cell."

"It should've been there. I know she had it on her."

"I'm sorry. It's not there."

"Look again."

"Joss..."

"Never mind. I'll find it myself. I forgot to add that I want Swan's car keys. I get my permit this summer, and it's only fair that I get her car."

"I didn't see the keys, either," I tell her.

"Jewell or Asher must have them," she says. "Did you look around the house?"

I did, but not for Swanee's car keys. "No." A half-truth.

"Look in Jewell's purses."

"Joss, I'm not about to go through Jewell's belongings. Or Asher's."

The pout on her face carries long-distance.

"Well, that car is mine, and so is everything else of Swan's. She was my sister. Mine." Joss's voice cracks and she ends the call.

Damn. I didn't call to upset her. I just needed to ask more questions about Liana.

My cell chirps. Same number. I answer and Joss says, "Check Jewell's red leather hobo bag for the cell and keys. She had it with her at the hospital."

Joss's voice is steady and demanding. I don't want to get into it with her again, but I'm not going to scrounge through Jewell's purses.

"Can I ask you a couple more questions about Liana?"

Joss goes, "God. Can't you just drop it?"

"How long did they go together?"

Joss says, "I suck at math."

I grit my teeth. "I don't. Tell me when they met and I'll do the math."

"I don't know the exact date."

"Approximately."

She expels an exasperated breath. "Approximately August fifteenth."

"Of last year?"

"No. Nineteen eighty-four."

I ignore that. "How do you know?"

"I was there. It was during freshman orientation, and Swan volunteered to be my senior escort. We had this overnight camping trip in Estes Park, and Greeley West was having a cheerleading camp there at the same time. I guess their gaydars crossed."

August fifteenth was two weeks before school started. "Wasn't Swanee going with Rachel the first month of school or so?"

"Swan dumped her in October," Joss says.

I hate that expression. "So Swanee and Liana didn't start going out until after?"

Joss lets out a short laugh.

"What?"

"You might be good at math, but you suck at logic. Why do you think Swan gave Liana a fake name?"

I'm . . . stunned.

"Does that answer all your questions?" Joss says. "Aren't you glad you asked?" She ends the call.

Mom opens my door and says, "What are your plans for the day?"

Sleep. I didn't sleep all night, processing what Joss had told me. If Liana was the reason Swanee broke up with Rachel, does that make me "the other woman," too? Joss said Swan and Liana were over, but were they? Liana's text messages suggest otherwise.

"Alix?"

I'm still speechless.

"Your dad and I would like to go to a movie and were wondering if you'd mind babysitting."

That word jolts me back to reality. "I can't. Betheny asked me to help her with this . . . um . . . project."

Mom looks at me—through me—and smiles. "Tell Betheny she's welcome to come over and work on it here. I miss her. I've been wondering what happened between the two of you."

"Nothing happened." Swanee happened. I add, "We have to do it at her house because it's on her desktop." Where do I come up with this crap? Who uses a desktop anymore?

"Do you think Betheny would mind if you took Ethan with you?"

"Mom, we wouldn't get anything done. He's a total distraction."

Her smile dissipates. "Fine. We won't go."

A knot of guilt forms in my stomach because they never go out together. "Can't you call Jennifer?" She's the owner of the day care where Ethan goes.

"I did. She's busy. We'll just go to the children's museum. Again."

Guilt-trip overload.

I can't babysit. The last time I did, I almost killed my baby brother. It was that day Mom and Dad left me and Swanee alone with Ethan. Swan was watching *Pirates of the Caribbean* for, like, the fifth time, and I was bored, so I had all my jewelry makings spread all over the floor.

It seems Swanee wasn't as into the movie as I thought because as soon as Mom and Dad left, she pushed me over and started kissing me. She had her hand up my shirt, tracing the outline of my bra and sticking fingers inside, and it felt so good, and I was losing control and just about to push her off when Ethan started choking.

His lips were turning blue and he was gasping for air and I freaked. I dug in his mouth but couldn't feel anything, so I bent him forward over my arm and began to pound his back. Hard enough to crack a rib, but I was panicking.

"Call 911," I told Swanee.

She just sat there.

All at once an object flew out of Ethan's mouth and he drew a deep breath. As if in reflex, he began to wail. I lifted him up and carried him around the room, trying to calm him. I'd never seen him cry so hard.

I warmed a bottle and he finally settled back in my lap, but I couldn't stop shaking.

"What did he swallow?" I asked Swanee.

She got up and found a slimy button on the carpet. All I could think was, I'm so irresponsible, I'm so irresponsible.

And Swanee... She wanted to pick up where we left off.

After that Ethan always looked terrified whenever I came close. Like he knew he was in imminent danger.

I take a shower to wash the memory away, and it helps. A little. Lying on my bed, I log on to Facebook and see that no new condolences have been left on my wall. I don't know if I'm thankful or not. It's like Swanee's being forgotten, and it's only been two weeks.

There is a message waiting for me.

It's from Liana. One sentence: I don't understand

She must've seen the few photos in my album, and read my relationship status. I message Liana back: She lied to you. I almost add, She lied to both of us, but I have this revelation: What if Swanee *did* break up with Liana and Liana couldn't, or wouldn't, accept it? She might've been stalking Swanee. Swan never mentioned it to me, but maybe she didn't figure it was my problem. Or she ran out of time.

I go to unfriend Liana and see she's already responded to my message.

We need to talk. Call me?

She's included her phone number.

I don't want to call her. Now I just want her to go away, to never have existed. There's nothing and no one who can fill this void that's expanding inside me day by day. Knowing Swanee's past will only make the present more real.

I go to log off and see another message has arrived.

It's her again. Please?

Shit. Why did I start this? Now I'm obligated to end it.

I nearly make the mistake of using Swanee's cell. Liana answers my call on the first ring. I say, "This is Alix."

She inhales and exhales a stuttered breath. "I can't believe she's dead." Liana barely gets the words out before she hiccups a sob. "I found her obituary online, and the date matched the one you said."

Her pain travels through me, and my eyes pool.

"Did you know Joss was texting me all this time?" she asks

I cringe. "No."

She starts sobbing again.

There's no way we're going to be able to talk on the phone. I say, "Do you want to meet?"

She blows her nose. "I have to work at two."

"Where do you work?"

"In Greeley. At the mall."

I check my clock and it's a little after ten. Mom and Dad will probably be gone until early afternoon.

"We could meet now," I say.

"Where?" She sniffles.

"I don't know."

"There's a McDonald's in Broomfield right off 287. Do you know where that is?"

"Yeah," I say.

She adds, "It'll probably take me twenty or twenty-five minutes."

"If I get there first, I'll wait." I owe her that.

She stays on the line, like she wants to say more. Or is waiting for me to speak. This sensation floods through me like when a roller coaster begins its ascent and you can see the top of the rise and you know any second the bottom is going to drop out from under you.

She starts crying again and disconnects. I hang on a moment longer, regaining my equilibrium.

Chapter 9

For some reason I take my time getting ready. Combing my hair into a ponytail the way Swanee usually wore hers, and then taking it down. As if it might remind Liana. As if I care. Putting on makeup. Trying different outfits.

"For God's sake," I say aloud. "It's not a date."

When I get to the McDonald's, she's huddled in a corner booth, hugging her knees, her face buried between her arms. There's a Coke cup with a straw on the table in front of her, but nothing else. I approach and she lifts her head slowly. Her face looks drained and her eyes are red.

I slide in across from her and she hides her face again.

This is going to be a waste if she's not even going to talk to me. Suddenly, she twists her head so her cheek is resting on her knee and says, "When did you know?"

Know what? Oh. "The day she . . . it . . . happened."

Liana's eyelashes are wet and she wipes a tear from under one eye. Blinking up at me, she says, "Why would she tell me her name was Swanelle Delaney and that she went to Cherry Creek High?"

I don't want to touch that. "Why does—did—Swan do anything?"

Liana doesn't seem to register the remark. She looks off, out the window. "I called her Swan, too."

Oh, God. I fight for control over my emotions.

"Did she even live in Greenwood Village?"

"No," I say. "She lived in Arvada and went to Arvada High." My stomach rumbles and I say, "I need something to eat or drink."

Liana shoves her Coke across the table. "Take mine. I haven't touched it. I'll buy you something if you're hungry. And pay for your gas, since I made you come."

"That's okay. You didn't make me." It's nice of her to offer. I don't want her to be nice. I want her to be a stalker. And a bitch. But I do accept the Coke.

The cold, fizzy liquid feels soothing to my dry throat as I sip from the straw. She watches me intently with her big brown eyes and says, "Joss always hated me. Swan said she was prejudiced against Mexicans. But it goes beyond prejudice to text me for so long after Swan was gone and make me think she was still alive. That's just cruel."

I choke. Set the cup down.

I've never known Joss to be racially biased. She pretty much loathes people across the board.

I open my mouth to tell Liana it was me, and I'm sorry, and I don't know why I did it except I wasn't in my right mind at the time.

"I didn't even get to say a rosary for her." Liana swallows hard. "Did she have a service?"

I nod. "More like a party."

Liana frowns. "Why would you have a party when someone passes?"

My question exactly. "Jewell and Asher wanted to celebrate her life."

"Who are they?"

Is she serious? "Swanee's parents."

Her eyes widen. "You know them?"

"Yeah. They're cool."

She just looks at me. "I don't get any of this. Swan lies about her name and where she lives and goes to school. She tells me her parents don't know she's gay—"

I laugh a little. Liana's eyes harden. "They knew," I say. "She's the outtest person in the world."

Liana's head drops back against the seat. I swirl the straw in the Coke and look at her. She's beautiful, even though she's wrung out. Liana lifts her head. "It says on your Facebook profile that you were in a relationship with her."

I can't hold her eyes. "I was."

"For how long?"

"Since Christmas break." I should've cherished every moment like it was our last. You never think... "How long were you with her?"

Liana watches me draw Coke from her straw. "The twentieth of February would've been our six-month anniversary. We were planning to get married after graduation."

I cough and Coke comes up my nose. "Joss said she broke up with you."

"Joss is a liar, in case you haven't figured that out by now." In a murmur she adds, "A heartless liar with no soul." She pauses. "I assume you found out about me through her. She must've been jumping with joy to let you know Swan was cheating on you."

The statement strikes me like a blow to the chest.

I say, "It wasn't like that. I found clues. Stuff in Swan's room. Your poetry book and your CD. I had to drag it out of Joss."

"Right," she says, like she doesn't believe me.

Our eyes meet again.

Liana's well with tears. "I can't do this." She slides out of the booth and races to the exit.

I'm paralyzed. Not only was Swanee dating Liana behind my back—cheating—she told me I was the love of her life and that we would always be together.

My cell rings on my way home, but I know better than to answer while I'm driving. The ringtone indicates it's Mom or Dad, so no emergency, other than checking up on me. I hope to God they didn't call Betheny's house.

I pull into the garage and check my voice mail. It's Mom telling me they'll be home around five and to please figure out something for dinner.

Swanee never had to cook dinner for her family. I don't know of one time they even ate dinner together as a family.

Swanee.

I'm so baffled now I'm not even sure who's lying to who. If Swanee had given Liana her real name, she'd have known about Swanee's death. I wonder if Swan gave a single thought to how much pain it would cause both Liana and me if either of us found out about the other.

Why I care about Liana's feelings is a mystery. Except I know how much I've been hurting since Swanee died, and I'd only been going with her for a few weeks. We hadn't even slept together.

Mom calls again and I answer, feeling numb. She says, "Did you get my message?"

"Yes." Marching orders received.

"How was Betheny's?"

"Fine," I say.

"Did you finish the project?"

Rather than lying, I say, "I better get started on dinner. Do you care if it's edible?"

I hear amusement in her voice when she replies, "You're a great cook and you know it."

At least I like to cook. Betheny and I used to watch the Food Network a lot, so I've developed a small repertoire of recipes. I find a package of frozen chicken breasts, which I microwave to thaw, and all the makings for panko-crusted chicken and scalloped potatoes. After I assemble everything and get it in the oven, I realize I'm starving. I grab a bag of Double Stufs to take to my room.

Swanee loved Oreos. We had this sexy way of eating them where she'd separate the halves, take a long lick of the frosting, and then hand it off to me to do the same. We'd repeat this until all the frosting was gone. Then she'd cover her eyes with the cookies and say, "Kiss me, Cookie Monster."

I almost laugh at the memory, but it lodges in my throat.

I make myself a PB-and-banana sandwich for lunch and throw in a handful of Oreos. Then I take the Oreos out and stack them back in the package.

At school, as I'm about to enter the media center to eat, the librarian is locking the door.

"Oh, Alix," she says. "You can't eat lunch in here every day. I thought you understood that."

I did, of course. I do. It's the rule.

I could eat in the restroom, I guess. How gross. As I trail a herd of students into the cafeteria, I see my regular spot is empty—the place where Swanee and I used to take up residence. Someone has even confiscated the chairs and left the table deserted. I look around as if I'm seeing the cafeteria for the first time. How all the cliques sit together. The jocks and the cheerleaders, the stoners, the loners, the Hispanics, the blacks. How depressing. So much for diversity training.

I hear the gays laughing and joking around, and I know I could go sit with them. But I haven't been to the GSA in so long I sort of feel like an outsider now. Raucous laughter a few tables over draws my attention. Betheny's eyes catch mine and hold. I wish I could go back in time to when we were BFFs. She glances away before I can even toss her an offhanded smile. That bridge went up in flames because of me. Relationships can't be reconstructed from ashes.

I can't stay here. I go to my locker, take out my coat, and eat outside at one of the picnic tables where all the smokers gather.

My fourth period is English and Mrs. Burke assigns a persuasive paper on the topic "Ignorance Is Bliss." I'm so distracted I miss the part where she asks for volunteers to take sides so we can discuss it next week. "Alix," she says, "would you mind taking the opposite position?"

I'm jolted awake by the sound of my name. "Which is what?" I ask her. Ignorance is ignorance?

"Yeah," someone else says. "What is opposite?"

"You'll figure it out," Mrs. Burke says.

Ignorance is bliss is easy. Until I knew about Swanee's death, I was ignorant of the true depth of pain a person could suffer.

Like Liana. She had two more weeks thinking Swan was alive. Maybe what I did wasn't so horrible. Saving someone the agony of loss can't be all bad.

Back home, as I'm lying in bed listening to music, my cell rings. No ID. It must be Joss, calling to ask if I've found Swanee's cell.

When I answer, Liana says, "I assume you know where Swan lives." She sounds pissed off. She has no right to be mad at me; I didn't do anything—that she's aware of. In fact, if I'd known about her, I never would've started dating Swanee. That's not the kind of person I am.

"Would you take me there?" It's more an order than a request.

So that means she was never in Swanee's room? Never stayed the night? It's a stretch, but maybe they didn't do it?

"Alix?"

I'm torn. I understand her needs, and wish I didn't. She has to touch and smell and sense what's left of Swanee. If I were selfish, I'd say no, what's left of Swanee is mine. But what does it matter now?

She adds, "We don't have to go inside or anything. I just want to see how far her lies extended."

How far is heartbreak and back?

"If you don't want to—"

"It's no problem," I cut in.

"When are you free?" Liana asks.

"Whenever." It sounds like I have no life. Which I don't.

"How about now? As soon as I can get there? I could meet you at Arvada. I'd like to see her real school, too."

"Okay. That'd work."

"I'll be driving a red Jetta," she says.

We disconnect and I link to her Facebook page. Just to remind myself what she looks like. As if that's necessary. Liana could be a supermodel.

Chapter 10

Her Jetta is already parked in the lot when I enter. I park next to her, but she doesn't get out. I open my door and circle her car. She rolls down her window.

"Do you want to follow me, or are you legal to drive other people by yourself?" I ask. Because there are laws.

"I can drive," she says. "Get in."

As I'm latching my seat belt, she adds, "I'll drop you back here afterward so you can pick up your car."

Without even thinking, I say, "It's my dad's car. I don't have my own."

"Oh. Okay."

She probably thinks I'm deprived by not having a car—which I am. No life. No car. No nothing. "I live close enough to walk to school." On rare days Swanee would finish her run in time to pick me up. She'd park a block away from my house, and when I saw her pink Smart car, a rush of excitement would flow through me. Thinking about it now, it feels as fresh as yesterday.

"Thanks for doing this, Alix. I know I'm being a pain."

"It's fine." I wish she'd drop the nice act. I can handle her bitchiness better, since she has every reason to resent me. We drive out of the lot and I say, "Take a left." She shifts gears and I ask, "Did you and Swan always meet at your house, then?"

Liana blinks at me and shakes her head. "My parents didn't like her, and vice versa. She met them a couple of times and said they gave off hater vibes."

My jaw drops. "That's the same thing she said to me."

Liana meets my eyes. "At least she was consistent."

I almost laugh, and then realize it's not funny. Liana can't be nice *and* funny.

We head to Swanee's cul-de-sac and Liana says, "Can I ask you a question? It's been bugging the hell out of me. I shouldn't say *hell*, but what the hell?"

I can't help cracking a smile. "Sure."

"Why would Swan pose as someone else? She had to jump through a lot of hoops to keep her real identity a secret. Because the more I think about it, the more I wonder if everything she told me about herself was a lie."

Why am I the one who has to end up hurting her again and again? "She was going with someone else when she met you. She didn't want either of you to find out."

I hear a small intake of breath. Liana goes, "Did she break it off with this other girl?"

I tell her the truth. "Yeah. In October."

Liana turns slowly and stares at me.

I can't look her in the eye. I lower my head. "I'm really sorry."

"Why? It's not your fault." She looks away.

No, it's not. So why do I feel like shit?

"I was wondering..." Liana lets out a long breath. "I'm trying to pick up some extra hours at work to pay for the engagement ring, since I charged it on my sister's MasterCard."

"Engagement ring?"

"We bought engagement rings for each other."

But Swanee would've taken it back after she met me. Right? Right?

"I went ahead and gave her mine at Christmas, but she wanted to keep hers on layaway until she could pay it off."

Liana sounds furious, the way I feel, or felt. I can't even begin to fathom this depth of deception.

"Anyway," she says, "I want my ring back."

I don't blame her.

"Have you seen a diamond ring in her room? She probably hid it from her parents. Or maybe she flaunted it, if what you say is true."

I shoot her a dirty look. Why would she have reason to doubt me? She doesn't know about my texting her, and she never will.

"Turn right here," I say. We pull into the cul-de-sac and I tell Liana to park at the curb behind Genjko's van. There's no danger of us blocking him in, since all four of his tires are flat, not to mention he's still in Hawaii, as far as I know.

I get out and shut my door, and then head up the sidewalk. Liana's not behind me. I go back and lean down to the window. She cracks it open an inch. "Are you coming?" I ask.

"I don't want to meet her family."

"They're not home. They went to Hawaii."

She gives me that same bewildered look Mom did.

"Hang on." I walk to the porch and ring the doorbell. A minute passes and no one answers. I signal to Liana to come.

She seems reluctant to approach the house. I find the key under the frog and open the door. It's cold inside. Freezing. Maybe I should've turned up the thermostat the last time I was here.

Liana stands outside, peering in through the doorway.

"It's not haunted," I say. But my eyes stray to the urn of ashes and I wonder.

Liana finally steps inside so I can close the door. Her eyes dart around. "Huh," she says. "It's definitely not what I expected."

That makes sense. If Swanee said she lived in Greenwood Village, Liana would expect a mansion.

"She said her parents were loaded—like country-club types. Which is one reason she couldn't come out to them. Their reputations, you know?"

That makes me laugh out loud. "Asher fixes foreign cars, and Jewell works part-time as a caretaker for a man with Alzheimer's."

Liana's big eyes narrow.

"Do you want to see her room?"

Liana shrugs one shoulder. "I guess so. It'd be nice to find that ring so I don't have to work my butt off for the rest of my life."

On the way down the hall, I ask, "Where do you work?"

"Victoria's Secret."

A visual of her in a skimpy bra and a thong flashes through my mind, and I get this little thrill. Feeling ashamed, I push it down. Swanee owned a ton of provocative underwear. Did Liana use her employee discount to buy it all for her?

I never thought I'd be back here, and I wish I weren't. But I suppose after so many lies, Liana deserves as much truth as Swanee's room will reveal. "It's here." I point to the closed door.

She hesitates the way I did, maybe hoping this is all a dream and Swan will emerge. Liana clasps the handle and turns it slowly. Inside, emptiness. She enters, while I sit cross-legged just outside the threshold.

I try to see the room through Liana's eyes. There are rainbow buttons and stickers all over Swan's mirrors. The Johnny Depp posters. The bag from the hospital on the bed.

"What are all the trophies for?" Liana asks.

"Track and field," I say. I'm surprised Swan didn't tell her that, at least. But then I realize Liana could've looked it up. "She was a runner. Last year she won the sixteen-hundred and thirty-two-hundred meters at State, and raced in the relays. She was practicing for the upcoming season when..."

I wonder if Liana's thinking the same thing I am: How does a person who's in phenomenal shape just drop dead? Don't they have to get sports physicals?

Liana picks up the essay notebook. "I wrote these poems to her," she says, more to herself than to me. "I put my heart and soul on these pages." She opens the cover and flips through it. "There are pages missing."

The ones I tore out in my fit of rage. "If it makes you feel any better," I say, "she kept it right there on her nightstand."

Liana turns and meets my eyes. "Here's how it makes me feel." She rips out the rest of the pages and flings them across the room. She throws the notebook like a Frisbee and it clunks against the opposite wall. Picking up a sweatshirt, she shakes it out. It's the blue one I rolled up to rest my head on. The back reads UNIVERSITY OF NORTHERN COLORADO IN GREELEY. "This is mine," she snarls. She hugs it to her chest, then kicks through the junk on the floor and grabs the necklace with the cross off the desk. "This is mine, too." She digs through the rest of the crap on the desktop, and then clears it with a swipe of her arm. "Where's the ring? I know you know where it is."

My cheeks flush. "I don't! I swear."

She charges toward me like she's going to kick me and take me down, but she vaults over my body instead. A moment later, I hear the front door shut.

Bitch, I think. The least you could've done is take me back to school.

As I'm locking the front door behind me, I see Liana sitting in her car, her forehead pressed to the steering wheel. Waiting for me? When I head down the walk, she guns the motor and tears off.

That night I call Joss and ask when they're coming home.

"Soon, I hope," she says. "I hate this fucking family, if that's what you even want to call it. Every minute with them is like living in the fiery pit of hell."

Always the drama queen. "But you don't know when?"

"Why? Do you miss me?"

When I don't answer right away, Joss laughs bitterly.

I don't want to go back in Swanee's room. Not ever. But I may have to. "Do you know where the engagement ring that Liana gave Swanee is?"

"The what!"

She sounds genuinely shocked. "Swan didn't tell you they were engaged?"

"No way. Who told you that?"

"Liana."

"Why are you talking to her?"

I'm not going to tell Joss we're trading war stories and basically trashing her sister. "So you never saw a ring?"

"There's no fucking ring. Swan would've shown me." Joss clicks her tongue. "Engaged. I'm so sure. Have you found the cell or car keys?"

"No. Sorry."

"You better, because Jewell is threatening to put a lock on Swan's door." She ends the call.

The way she reacted, I believe Joss didn't know about the engagement. Now I have all these doubts floating around in my head again. I know Swanee lied to Liana about her identity, but now I wonder if Liana's lying to me about the engagement. To make *me* feel worse? Or more inadequate than I already do? I try to put myself in her shoes and can't. Her six months trumps my six weeks.

I feel a connection with Liana that I wish I didn't. Not only did Swan lie to both of us, in her wake she left a path of emotional devastation.

* * *

I open a blank document to start my persuasive paper and key in the title: "Ignorance Isn't Ignorance." That can't be right. A wall goes up and I don't want to scale it, or even figure out the topic of this paper.

I link to my Facebook page and see that I have a message; it's from Liana. My stomach does a little flip. Maybe she's going to ask for forgiveness. She doesn't even realize what it took for me to willingly share Swanee with her.

The message reads: I can't be your friend. Sorry.

I check out my friends list and see that she's no longer there. It's not like we ever were friends, really, but no one's ever unfriended me. Not even Betheny.

Chapter 11

I wake to the smell and sound of bacon sizzling downstairs. My nose leads me to the kitchen, where Dad's fixing Sunday breakfast. Mom's there, feeding Ethan a bowl of watery baby cereal. Her beeper goes off and she curses under her breath. She says to me, "Would you mind?" Meaning taking over the feeding. That I can do, as long as other people are around in case I screw up. I slide into her chair as she hurries to the phone to call the hospital.

Dad sets a plate of eggs, hash browns, and bacon in front of me.

"Thank you." I rub my hands together. "I'm starving."

He plants a kiss on the top of my head. If I hadn't felt it, I wouldn't have believed it.

Mom hangs up and says, "I'm sorry. I have to go." She hustles over to Dad and gives him a peck on the cheek. Slowing behind me, she pats my shoulders. "How are you doing, sweetie?"

Is there an answer to that? "Okay."

Dad sits down with his plate and says to me, "What's on your agenda for today?"

Sleeping. Zoning. "Nothing. Why?"

"I thought we'd all go tubing at Winter Park."

"Seriously?" My spirits lift. We haven't done that since I was a kid.

"Depending on how long your mom has to work."

I slump. She'll be there for hours, and by then it'll be too late to drive to the mountains.

Ethan clamps his lips together every time I lift the spoon to his mouth. Like he's afraid I'm going to poison him. Meanwhile, my eggs and bacon are congealing. I give up on Ethan and dig into my breakfast, and Ethan lets out a bloodcurdling scream.

"Alix," Dad says.

"Well, he won't let me feed him."

Dad scoots his chair down to take over, and suddenly Ethan is all smiles. It hurts that he hates me. What'd I ever do, except nearly kill him?

After eating and cleaning up, I go to my room and dig Dad's old fishing-lure box out of the closet. I sit on my floor to make jewelry. In the box are rolls of colored wire and dental floss, beads of every shape and size, old buttons I've collected over the years. I have squares of colored paper for origami, along with posts and gold loops. There's an earring on top that I started and never finished. It's braided wire with colored beads in the order of a rainbow: red, orange, yellow, green, blue, purple.

It was for Swanee, of course. I don't know why I kept making them for her when she never wore them. Except she did always say she loved them.

I can't finish this one; I can't even stand to look at it. I set it aside. The buttons I've collected over the years have come from clothes I bought at thrift stores and Goodwill. I sort through them for a matched pair to make earrings for someone—maybe Jewell. She wears lots of beads and bangles. Or Joss. I feel guilty about not defending her to Liana.

Joss texts me around nine AM to tell me they're home AT LAST!!!! She asks if she can come over. I text her that we're going to Winter Park today.

She texts:

Can I go?

I don't want her to. Not today.

I lie:

Dad says he wants it to be just family

A minute later she texts back:

Then can you drop me off at a friend's before you leave?

I can do that.

Sure

Mom's still at the hospital, and Dad's in the living room, giving Ethan a bottle. "I need to run out for a minute," I tell Dad.

He glances up. "How long's a minute?"

I mock sneer at him. "Like, half an hour."

"No more than an hour," he says. "And if your mom gets home early, we'll call you."

I take the keys and dash to the garage. When I ring the bell at the Durbins', Joss answers.

"Hi," I say. "How was your trip?"

"Awesome," she deadpans.

Genjko passes behind her with his duffel and heads for his room, giving off an aura of live ammo. Lost his Zen, I guess.

"We're outta here," Joss mutters.

Jewell snags Joss's sleeve. "Where are you going?"

Joss scowls. "None of your business."

"Hi, Jewell," I say as her cell rings. She ignores me to answer it.

Asher's cell bleeps and he disappears into the living room. A moment later he reappears and says, "I have to go out for a while."

Joss follows me to the porch. "And we all know why."

Why? I wonder.

Jewell's car emerges from the garage.

As her parents head off in opposite directions, Joss says, "I don't know how they waited this long."

My eyes ask the question, and Joss answers, "They have an open marriage."

I must look flabbergasted.

Joss smirks. "Mommy and Daddy have fuck buddies." She studies my face as if to gauge my reaction. I try my hardest to regain some sort of impassivity.

Swan never mentioned that, but then it's something that wouldn't come up in casual conversation. She might've been embarrassed. I know I would've been.

Joss says, "My own fuck buddy awaits."

I think, She's kidding, right? She's barely fifteen—not old enough to have sex. But then, how old is old enough? I sort of wish I'd done it earlier so I won't be a virgin the rest of my life.

She gives me directions, and as we're driving she pulls out a cell. I see her text OMW, for "on my way." Whatever he texts back makes Joss giggle. I wonder if whoever she's seeing got her the phone. It's actually a relief; maybe she'll stop bugging me about Swan's phone.

When she disconnects, I say, "Will you please look in Swan's room for a ring?"

Joss's voice hardens. "I told you. There. Is. No. Ring."

We drive for fifteen minutes, and then half an hour, and more. "Where are we going?" I ask. Because this is longer than the quick trip I expected.

"Right here." She points to the entrance of a trailer park. "Stop." She unfastens her seat belt and opens the car door.

The guy who's waiting in the doorway looks at least thirty. Isn't it illegal to date a minor? And if they're having sex, that's statutory rape.

God, Joss, I think. Aren't you in enough trouble?

Before I can ask if she'll need a ride home—like, *right now*—she's ushered inside and the door shuts behind her.

At home I remote open the garage door and see that Mom's back from the hospital. It's after eleven, too late to drive to Winter Park. "Where have you been? I've been calling you," she snaps as soon as I walk through the door.

If Joss's "friend" hadn't lived in Kansas...If I'd been

thoughtful enough to call . . . I go to fish my phone out of my bag, but grab Swanee's instead.

"Whose cell is that?" Mom asks.

I drop it back in my bag and avoid her eyes, and the question, while I'm searching for my phone. I have voice mail. "My cell's dead," I lie. "I forgot to charge it."

"You didn't answer my first question." Mom holds out her hand.

I'm not giving her Swanee's cell. "It's Betheny's. She left it in the cafeteria on Friday, and I picked it up to give it back to her." This sense of Swanee envelops me. Once you start to lie, it's hard to stop. In fact, it almost becomes a game.

Just then my cell vibrates. Shit. I glance at the caller ID and it's not a number I know offhand. A knot of resentment forms in my chest because I'm not Joss's chauffeur. Then I feel bad because I should get my ass over there and save her. I shrug at Mom, like I don't know how my phone magically recharged itself. "Hello?" I answer, walking around Mom and toward the stairs.

Liana says, "It's me. You can hang up if you want to."

My pulse races. "Oh, hey, Betheny," I say. "Yeah, I have your cell. Can I bring it over later? We're going to Winter Park."

I check with Mom for confirmation and she shakes her head no.

"Or I could do it after I'm ungrounded for life."

Liana doesn't respond. She must think I'm crazy.

"My mom says hi." I lope up the stairs, adding, "He did? Cool."

Liana disconnects. I want to call her back so badly and find out why she called.

I start to dial, but can't. We shouldn't be in contact. Obviously, Swanee didn't want us to know about each other, and I think she'd be freaked to find out we'd met.

Score one for us.

Why does it matter what Swanee might've thought? I just don't want Liana to think... whatever she does at the moment. I don't get her, though. Why does she unfriend me and then call? I send her a text:

Sorry about that. My mom was standing right there

I key:

Do you want something?

Duh. She wouldn't have called otherwise. I delete that line and try to think what else to say. Nothing comes to mind, so I press Send.

She doesn't text back. I wait five, ten minutes. Mom comes upstairs and opens my door. "I'm going to lie down for a while. Your dad might conk out in front of the TV, so if Ethan wakes up, would you mind giving him a bottle?"

If he'll take it from me. Which he won't.

"I need to go to Betheny's," I say, "and drop off her cell."

"Why can't she come here?"

"She's... grounded."

"Betheny?" Mom arches her eyebrows.

Think fast. "She's been so busy with cheerleading and all her clubs that her grades have dropped."

"Which reminds me." Mom folds her arms. "I looked online at your grades and noticed you didn't turn in several assignments. And you missed five days of school in January. I don't know why the school didn't call your father or me."

"Their records are wrong." In fact, Swan called in for me, pretending to be my mother. She'd perfected her "authoritative" voice over the phone. I remember this one prank call she made....

Mom's looking at me like she doesn't believe a word of it. She goes on, "I can understand how difficult these last few weeks have been for you, but please don't let your schoolwork suffer."

A lump clogs my throat. She must see that I can't explain. I can, but the reason is sitting in an urn on a mantel.

She relaxes her arms. "I'm sorry we didn't get to go to Winter Park today."

I pick up my backpack and unload a pile of books on my bed. "Doesn't matter. You're right. I have a ton of homework."

Mom says, "If you need a break from studying, you can go to Betheny's. But just for a little while."

"Mom." I catch her before she leaves. "Don't athletes have to have physicals before they can participate in sports?"

She gives me a blank look before she understands what I'm asking. "They do," she says, "but ventricular fibrillation, which is the usual cause of sudden cardiac arrest, may not be detected in sports physicals. I think the rules are changing to be more thorough, but don't quote me on that."

Before closing the door, she adds, "Sometimes it's just out of our hands."

Chapter 12

I'll only be gone a couple of hours, and in the realm of eternal salvation, who marks time?

I almost miss her red car as I drive past it in the rear of the mall lot. I feel happy she's here. Why? Probably because if she wasn't I would've driven to Greeley for nothing.

The mall is almost empty because it's Sunday. I head down the center aisle—the only aisle—through a seating area where a couple of older people are reading newspapers and drinking coffee.

As I approach Victoria's Secret, I slow. In my head I have it all worked out, what I'll say:

"Hi. You called me?"

She'll be shocked to see me in person. Or will she? Do people go running to her whenever she beckons?

"Did you want to say something?" I'll ask.

Because we've said everything there is to say. Haven't we?

She'll go, "No." She'll lower those big brown eyes and

look embarrassed. Or be triumphant that she's yanked my chain.

I'll say...

I haven't worked out the rest of the conversation.

She's inside the store, near the front, not doing anything. Just gazing out into the mall. I duck behind a bank of gumball machines across from the store, feeling like an idiot.

She didn't notice me, I don't think. She stands there with this blank expression on her face, her eyes glazed over. A bolt of anguish shoots straight through me: She's coming to terms with Swan's death.

The most I've ever done is window-shop at Victoria's Secret and wish I had the guts to go inside and browse.

It takes every ounce of willpower I have to force my feet to move, to step out from around the gumball machines and enter the store. Liana's eyes widen when she sees me.

"Hi," I say. I forget my next line; I have to improvise. "Would you help me? I'm looking for a gift for my great-aunt."

Liana says flatly, "Do you have something in mind? How old is she?"

I remove a red negligee from a nearby rack and hold it up. "She turns eighty-five tomorrow."

That coaxes a smile out of her.

"Liana, there's inventory to do as soon as you're done talking to your friend," a voice calls from the cash register.

Liana rolls her eyes and says under her breath, "My supervisor."

I call back, "I'm not a friend. I'm a customer."

"Oh. Excuse me." The supervisor skirts the counter with an armload of bras.

When she's out of earshot, I say, "I was thinking my great-aunt Wilma might like some lacy butt floss."

Liana shakes her head. "You're bad." She considers for a minute, and then says, "I have just the thing."

Do her eyes twinkle, or am I hallucinating? She leads me to a center rack, where a collection of corsets and babydolls hang. She takes one off the rack and shows it to me.

"Definitely Great-Aunt Wilma." It's leopard and lace with black garters.

Liana grins. "It's called a merry widow." Her eyes sort of lose their luster. After a long second, she says, "I dare you to put it on."

The mischievous glint is back. I take the lingerie from her and say, "Where's the fitting room?"

She points.

As I pass her supervisor, I smile sweetly.

The fitting room is ice cold and goose bumps rise on my skin, especially since I have to strip down to practically nothing to shimmy into the garment.

It's totally revealing. My butt cheeks and boobs hang out. A knock sounds on the door and Liana says, "How's it going in there?"

Dare I? I unlock the door and swing it open.

She eyes me up and down, making me feel even more naked than I am. Then she covers her mouth and starts to giggle. That makes me giggle, and I pull her inside the dressing room.

“I should make *you* try it on,” I say.

She can’t stop giggling.

“Shut up. Does it make me look fat?”

“No,” Liana says. “You look...” She swallows hard. Her face sobers and she glances away. “Can I ask, how did you and Swan meet?”

I want to change back into my regular clothes if we’re going to have a serious discussion, but she sits on the bench, facing me.

“On a ski trip over winter break,” I tell her. We’re close enough that I can feel her body warmth. “A friend of Swan’s was supposed to come, but she sprained her ankle.”

Liana blinks. “Ice-skating with her the week before. I fell and sprained my ankle.”

Cacophonies of consequences churn in my brain. What if Liana had gone to Winter Park? What if Swanee and I had never met? What if Swanee hadn’t died?

“Liana?” the supervisor calls.

Liana pushes to her feet. “Coming.” She pauses at the door and pivots around. Our eyes meet and hold. Instinctively, I cover up my exposed areas—or try to.

After she’s gone, I feel heat swelling from every pore, exposed and otherwise. She’s hot. Very hot.

I get dressed, take the lingerie out front and see that Liana’s busy with inventory or something. The supervisor’s at the cash register and I say to her, “I’ll take this.” I hand her my Visa, which I’m only supposed to use for necessities.

As I'm leaving the store, I stop behind Liana and watch her punch a number on her calculator. I say, "Thanks for your help, miss."

She turns and glances down at the bag. "You're getting it?"

"Everyone over eighty needs a merry widow."

She laughs. All the way home the resonance of her laughter radiates through me.

My persuasive paper is due tomorrow and all I've written so far is the title. Typically, before Swanee, I never put off assignments, unlike normal people. My MO is to obsess over unfinished business.

I set my laptop aside and lie back on my pillow. To think. Concentrate.

Liana might not be home from work yet. It's only, what? Seven thirty? Maybe she's working overtime.

I prop up my pillows again and pull my laptop over in front of me. If Liana doesn't call by ten, I'll call her. I'll say...

What? "Do you have any more questions? Ask me anything."

I can't compose a mental script when I'm supposed to be working on this stupid essay.

Ignorance is ignorance. It seems so simple, or redundant. So why am I having trouble defending it?

I wish I'd chosen the other side of the argument. Ignorance is bliss. Being kept in the dark and not having to deal with the truth is easy. It's denial. Swanee told me that Asher and Jewell declared bankruptcy last year. They refused to see, or admit, that they were living beyond their means.

I know Jewell's a shopaholic, and Swanee always got anything she wanted. For her sixteenth birthday, she got the Smart car. If she knew her family was in financial straits, would she have accepted the car? When did she learn they were having money problems? Did she try to give the car back? As much as I want a car, I know I'd be conflicted if my parents were struggling to put food on the table.

For my seventeenth birthday in November, I got a Visa. Big whoop. The monthly limit is so low that if I exceed it, which I do every month, Mom and Dad get on my case.

What time is it? I check my laptop clock. Almost eight.

I key in a couple of paragraphs about avoiding the pain and messiness of real life, keeping yourself emotionally safe. Ignorant. It sounds lame.

"The darker the shades, the easier life is on the eyes," I write.

Mrs. Burke is going to give me a flaming F.

What time is it now? Eight twenty. Close enough.

I dial Liana's number and it goes to voice mail. I don't know what to say, so I just hang up.

She obviously doesn't check her missed calls immediately the way I do. See? Obsessed.

An hour later I'm still staring at a silent cell.

I run through the events of today. We had a good time. At least I did, and she seemed to. We shouldn't be having fun, since we're both in mourning. But for some reason I think that creates a bond. Both of us being victimized by Swanee's lies.

I can't think of one more thing to add to this essay. All I can do is hope that a lot of people write crappy essays and that Mrs. Burke grades on a curve. That might earn me an F+.

Mom and Dad are in the living room with the lights off and the TV on. Dad's giving Mom a foot rub. As I snag Dad's keys, Mom cranes her neck over the sofa back and asks, "Are you going out?"

No, I just wanted to suck on the keys. "There's something I need at Swanee's. I know you told me not to go over there, but..." But what? I need to get out of here and clear my head.

"What is it?" Mom asks.

Swan still has jewelry that I gave her, not that I really want it back. I'd rather look for that ring. I tell Mom, "This T-shirt we made in GSA for Day of Silence." The lies are flowing freely again. The Swanee Effect.

Dad says, "It's too late to bother them on a Sunday night. Can't you stop by and pick it up in the morning?"

Mom adds, "I have a better idea. I'll call Jewell and ask her to drop it off on her way to work. What does it look like?"

"She can't go into Swanee's room, Mom."

Mom frowns. "Why not?"

Do I really have to tell her? "She just can't set foot in there."

That shuts Mom up.

"We'll work something else out," Dad goes.

Which means no. I storm back upstairs and almost slam my door. That, I know, would cost me, especially if I woke Ethan. Thankfully I stop myself and lose the attitude so my credit card limit doesn't dwindle to zero, or something worse.

I catch the glow of Swanee's cell in my bag and take it out. She has two texts from today. They're both the same number, but it's not Liana.

The first one reads:

if u have this cell ur a thief n im reporting u to the cops

The number looks familiar. I check Swanee's contacts and it's not in there. Then I think to check my cell. Aha. It's the number Joss has been using. I should've known.

The second text reads:

if u want to keep the cops out of it put the cell in an envelope and send it to this address

It's a rural address in Hudson; probably that trailer where I left her today.

She's not getting Swanee's cell. Just as I'm dropping it back in my bag, my cell rings. It's a text from Liana:

Sorry I missed your call. My mom always asks who I'm talking to and there's nowhere in this house I can have a private conversation

Now I'm not even sure why I called her.

I text:

I hear you. Not literally

She texts:

LOL. I can't believe you bought the merry widow

I text:

Hey, you're the one who picked it out. In fact, I'm wearing it right now. I made dinner in it for the rents and now I'm doing laundry

LMAO

I text:

Do you like working there?

It's OK. Better than Chuck E. Cheese's ☺

But you'd get free pizza there ☺

And salmonella. At VS I get to dream about girls in lingerie all day ☺

There's a lull in the conversation, like maybe we shouldn't be having it. Then she texts:

I know you're not supposed to speak poorly of the dead, but what Swan did was wrong and unforgivable. Except I'm Catholic, so I have to forgive her. I don't want to hate her. I did at first. Every lie I found out about was like a stab in the back. But I don't want to let hatred control my life

Swan never should've done what she did to Liana. Or Rachel. Or me. No, there's no comparison with them and me. I know in my heart that Swanee loved me. She just wanted to make sure I was fully committed to her before she broke it off with Liana.

One more day and she would've known.

Yeah, it hurts to find out she was seeing someone else at the same time we were coming together. But given the chance, I would've proven to Swanee that no one could love her as much as I did.

Liana texts:

I have to go

Before she disconnects, I text:

Wait

A pause.

What?

That's the question, I think. Why am I making her wait? She needs to get on with her life, and so do I.

I text:

Nothing. Never mind

Chapter 13

When I hand in my persuasive paper, Mrs. Burke scans the mostly empty page and then turns it over to see if I've continued on the back. She gets that same look on her face that Mom gets when she's disappointed in me. I almost say, Quality over quantity, right? I'm surprised teaching doesn't bring out the serial killer in more adults.

On my way home I pass Swanee's street and see the Smart car parked at the end of the cul-de-sac with a FOR SALE sign in the window. LIKE NEW. $18,500.

Oh my God. Joss.

Jewell's just pulling into the driveway as I'm walking away and she waves at me. She gets out, shoulders her hobo bag, and calls, "Hi, Alix. Come in for a cappuccino. It'll have to be quick, though."

I trail her inside, wondering how to ask if she's regrouped. Her hair is damp and pulled back in a ponytail.

The house looks the same, table piled high with papers

and magazines, clothes flung all over the place. It reeks of incense, like Genjko got a bulk deal. He should lay off that stuff.

Jewell unzips her leather boots and pads in stocking feet to the coffeemaker. I sit in my usual seat at the table. We don't converse. Usually she's so chatty, asking me about my life and just talking girl talk.

She sets my coffee in front of me and says, "Have you seen Swanee's cell phone?"

Blood rushes to my cheeks.

"I'm betting Joss stole it, even though she swears she didn't. She's such a little liar and thief. She was always taking money from my purse, and I know she's been rifling through Swanee's room. Did Swanee tell you about the time Joss downloaded a bunch of porn onto my computer? It got some virus and I had to take it to the geeks to fix. You should've seen how they looked at me."

Swan did tell me about it. She thought it was hysterical. Joss, not so much. It was a dare for Joss to do it. Even if she didn't want to participate in Swanee's pranks, or was afraid of the consequences, she would never say no to Swanee.

Jewell takes her coffee and moves behind me toward the hall.

"Jewell." I twist in my seat. "Can I ask you a question?"

She stops and checks her watch. "I have a hair appointment in twenty minutes."

"Um, did you know Swanee was seeing another girl?"

Jewell laughs. "Only one?"

I don't laugh. She lifts her cup to her mouth, sips, and

then licks foam from her upper lip. "I told Swanee she was too young to be serious about just one person. At her age, I had guys lined up. Girls, too." She winks.

I just look at her. Did she know about Liana?

She says, "It's not like you were engaged, Alix."

My heart heaves and a whirring sound fills my ears. I manage to croak out the question, "Would you mind if I went in Swanee's room one more time? She... she borrowed this book, and I need to get it back to the library."

Jewell sighs, like it's a huge imposition. "Just for a minute." She retrieves her bag and digs around for a set of keys. I follow her down the hall and see that a deadbolt has been installed on Swanee's door.

"I saw the For Sale sign on the Smart car. Are you not keeping it for Joss because of the porn thing?"

Jewell whirls around. "That car would *never* have gone to Joss. If she told you that, she was lying." A cell phone rings in Jewell's bag and she says, "I'll be back to lock up when you're done." She answers the cell, "Hi, baby," as she enters her room and shuts the door.

I just stare after Jewell, thinking, Who is this person? She's changed. Or maybe I've never seen through her outer layer before.

I rummage around in Swanee's drawers again, feeling for a ring box. It could be anywhere on her floor or desk, or behind books. If the ring had been on her finger while she was running, it'd be in the hospital bag. I feel around in there and come up empty.

Joss was right. There is no ring. Liana was lying, and now

it's possible that she was lying about a lot of things. All of it. That she and Joss and Swanee were in on it together and the joke was on me. I sit on Swan's bed, feeling disoriented. Dizzy. Automatically, to stop the motion, my fingers slide under her mattress.

What's this?

I stand and lift the mattress a few inches. Money. A lot of it. Mostly twenties. If I had to estimate, I'd say there was four or five hundred dollars there.

It makes me mad because I was the one who always had to pay whenever we went out. Even when Joss was with us, Swanee said she was broke, and would I mind charging it on my Visa? Of course I didn't mind. I loved her.

Jewell's door opens and closes. She calls, "Alix, are you almost through? I need to go."

I leave the money, even though I should take it as reimbursement.

Beside the bookcase I see a couple of library books, so I grab them, inadvertently knocking over a trophy. A mitten falls out of the trophy and I bend to pick it up. It's heavy, like something's inside the mitten.

I empty the contents into the palm of my hand and see it's a ring box. Liana wasn't lying. This boiling anger at Swanee simmers inside me. Is that what we were to you? Trophies to add to your collection?

Jewell says from the threshold, "Did you find the book?"

Ever so slowly, I turn, sliding the ring box into my pocket. "Two, actually. They're both overdue, but I'll pay the fines."

She doesn't even say thanks, or offer to pay me back.

As she's locking the door behind me, Jewell picks up

where she left off. "I told Swanee she should have fun. See a lot of people. At her age, there was absolutely no reason to be tied down. Not just to you—"

I'm nauseated. I can't even stand to look Jewell in the eye. Never have I felt such revulsion for a person. Before I say something I'll regret, I rush to the door.

"If Joss tells you she has Swanee's phone, you let me know."

The words are a blur. Near the Smart car, my stomach gives out and I hurl. I want to scream. I want God or someone to fill me in on what's right or wrong in this world, what's honorable and decent, because the way Jewell and Asher live their lives, the morals they taught their children, it's no wonder Swanee was the way she was. Even if I didn't know them that long, how naïve could I be? How stupid? Suddenly my parents look like demigods next to them.

Did Swanee ever really love me, or was it all just a sham?

I text Liana:

I found your ring. Maybe you can return it for a refund

She doesn't text back, so I curl into a ball on my bed and cover my head with my pillow. I wish I could stop thinking, stop feeling, just... stop. My phone rings and it's a text from Liana:

Thanks! Sorry, I didn't get your message earlier. We were in the semis for girls' basketball so we went to cheer at their game. And yeah, I do want it back

I text:

Do you want me to mail it?

NO!!! I didn't tell my mom and dad we were engaged

Engaged. I still can't believe it was real, even with the ring as proof. Does Liana believe it was? Why would Swanee hook up with me if she loved Liana enough to marry her?

Liana texts:

She probably planned to pawn the ring and keep the money

To add to the fortune under her mattress, I think.

Liana texts:

You okay?

Me? No. I hurt. My heart aches. I want to hate Swanee for duping me and Liana, but I can't seem to get there. My love for Swanee *was* real, and still is.

Liana texts again:

Alix, you there?

I text back:

Yeah, just working through some things

She texts:

Me too. I can't stop crying. One minute I'm sad, then mad, then confused and empty. I could go on

She doesn't have to.

She texts:

We won our game, yay, so I'll be cheering on Wed at the Denver Coliseum. Is Arvada playing?

I text:

Doubtful. We suck at everything but track

She texts:

Do you want to meet after the game? Maybe talking it out will help

My heart does a little flutter, even though I know she's probably just interested in getting her ring back.

Sure

She texts:

Since you don't have a car, why don't I just come to your house to pick you up? Unless you're not out to your parents and they might ask questions

I text:

No, they know I'm a lesbian. That's not a problem. What time?

It's a late game so it won't end until 10 or 10:30

Breaking curfew is a problem. If only my parents were more lenient, like... forget that.

I text:

See you then

Dad and Mom are both up, dressed for work, hustling to eat breakfast and feed Ethan before he goes off to day care.

"Can I help?" I ask.

They both gawk at me.

Mom says, "You can feed Ethan so I can finish my breakfast and get dressed."

I don't quite have the hang of scooping food into Ethan's mouth without losing most of it down his front, but eventually we get this rhythm going where he opens, I shovel, and then I wait for him to swallow before offering the next bite. The whole time he whimpers, like he can barely endure the torture of me doing this.

"Can I ask you a question?" I say to Mom and Dad.

"Uh-oh," Dad says. "I knew there was a catch. How much?"

I mock sneer at him. "I'd like to go out tomorrow night. Kind of late. After the girls' basketball finals downtown."

Dad arches his eyebrows. "Arvada's in the finals?"

"That'd be a miracle," I say. "The game won't end until around ten, so I might miss my curfew. Unless it's extended? Please, please, pretty please?"

Dad removes his waffle from the toaster. "Who are you going with if Arvada isn't playing?"

Well, it can't be Betheny, can it? "Someone," I say.

"Clears that up," Dad goes. "Do we know him?"

I just look at Dad. My pause in our feeding rhythm makes Ethan spit at me. I swear he did it on purpose.

Dad corrects himself. "Her, I mean."

I shake my head.

Dad eyes Mom across the table, and she says, "We'd like to meet her."

"We're not dating," I tell them. "She's just a friend."

Mom takes her plate to the dishwasher. "We still like to know your friends."

A fast hi and bye, I think. "So can I go?"

They don't answer. They're going to say no. Why did I decide to go the noble route? I could've just snuck out and they never would've known.

Mom says, "It's a school night."

"I know that."

Ethan's getting squirmy and his face is turning red, like he's ready to explode.

Dad asks, "Where are you going?"

For God's sake. "I don't know. We're taking a private jet to the Bahamas."

"Nice," Dad says. "Can I come?"

Could this be more lame? I open my mouth to tell them to just forget it, but Ethan lets out a shriek. He smashes his tray, propelling his dish into the air, where it flips and lands right on top of my head. A beat passes, and then Mom and Dad burst into laughter.

Oh, yeah. It's so funny.

Now I'll have to shower again and change clothes. I scoot back my chair and stand.

"Just for that," Dad says, "I think we should let her go."

What? I search out Mom. She's holding her stomach at the sink, gasping for air while she laughs.

Dad says to me, "The bell tolls at midnight. After that you turn into a pumpkin."

I almost say "pauper," but now's not the time to quibble about fairy tales.

Chapter 14

I feel giddy. Alive. I can't wait for ten o'clock. It's crazy, really. Liana is—was—my rival. I should despise her. But all I feel is excited to see her again, and now I'm wondering if Mom was right about me needing to get professional help.

After dinner, I lay out every conceivable outfit I own. No one's bought me a new wardrobe since the last time I tried on clothes. I look frumpy in jeans and a long sweater, nerdy in the button-down cardigan Mom got me for Christmas. I try on the merry widow and stand in front of my mirror. A little black eye shadow and I could pass for a hooker on the prowl. This is seriously demented. I shimmy into my skinny jeans and a long-sleeved top. The jeans are looser than they used to be. I don't have to suck in my gut to button them.

My cell rings.

"I can't come," Liana says.

My spirits sink.

"Can we make it another time?" she asks.

A small air bubble of hope rises. "Sure."

"It's just that all the games are starting late, and Dad wants me to follow the team bus back home."

"You don't have to explain," I say. But I'm glad it's not because she made plans with someone else. Which is none of my business anyway.

"I'm really sorry."

She sounds sincere.

"It's okay."

"No, it's not. I've been looking forward to it."

Seriously?

She pauses. "Do you like the ring?"

"I..." almost say I haven't looked at it. But of course I have. It's gorgeous. I'd die if anyone ever gave me something so beautiful and meaningful. "I haven't put it on," I tell her.

"Just testing," she says with a smile in her voice.

I think I passed. I hope I did.

She adds, "I'm free after Mass on Sunday. Is that good for you?"

"Yeah," I tell her. All I'm doing here is wasting away, physically and emotionally.

"Around eleven?"

It can't be soon enough.

On Sunday morning, I keep peeking out the living room curtains, waiting for her to arrive. Dad says, "Expecting someone?"

I don't want to tell him because he and Mom weren't too happy about her standing me up the other night. Not that she did. Like I told them, we're not dating.

The Jetta comes into view and, as she pulls to the curb, I sprint out the door.

She rolls down her window and I hand her the ring box. She tosses it into her glove compartment.

"Don't you want to make sure it's in there?" I say.

"I never want to see that fucking ring again. Sorry, God." She makes the sign of the cross. "Anyway, I trust you."

A pang of guilt stabs me where it hurts. She has no reason to trust me—especially if she knew about the texts.

She asks, "Do you want to go somewhere to eat? I saw a Chipotle on the way here, and I'm starving."

I'm suddenly starving, too. From the doorway, I hear, "Alix?"

It's Dad. "Would you mind meeting my dad?" I ask Liana. "Tell him we're taking your private jet to lunch in Paris."

She furrows her brow.

"Just say hi."

She gets out and accompanies me up the sidewalk.

On the porch I say in a rush, "ThisisLiana. Liana, Dad."

She extends her hand to shake. "Hi," she says.

Dad asks, "How do you know Alix?"

Oh, God, no. Liana looks at me and I save her. "It's a long story. We're going out. Be back in a while."

I could kick myself. "Going out" sounds a whole lot like a date.

Liana smiles at Dad. "Nice to meet you."

I sense Dad wants to say more, but I hurry Liana away.

We order two humongous burritos and find a table near the window without nearby neighbors who can hear every word we say. Not that we're speaking. We're both slamming down food like there's no tomorrow. Which, in our world, seems imminently possible.

I like that she's not self-conscious about pigging out. Swanee was a picky eater. She had to disassemble everything and remove what she didn't like.

Liana and I sip from our straws in unison, and swallow. I wonder who'll break the ice. Although it feels perfectly natural to sit here in silence and chow down.

"Where'd you find the ring?" she finally asks.

"In her room. In one of her trophies."

Liana rips off another bite of burrito between her teeth.

"You know how I told you Jewell and Asher were cool parents? I take it back. They're psycho." I tell Liana about what Jewell said to me, and how she encouraged Swan to basically sleep around.

Liana's eyes shoot flames and she shakes her head. "It doesn't excuse her behavior."

"No, I know. But maybe it explains it a little. Poor Joss." I take a bite of my burrito.

"What about Joss? She's going down with Swan for texting me."

Now would be the perfect time to tell Liana the truth, and I open my mouth to do it, but the words stick in my throat. Still, it isn't fair for her to hate Joss. "I think Joss is the most normal one of the bunch."

Liana scrunches up her nose. "How do you figure?"

"She's just trying to get attention," I say. "Plus, she did anything Swan told her to. Did you know about the porn?"

Liana's eyes grow wide. "The what?"

I tell Liana the story.

"The only thing I heard about was the naked text. Swan dared her to do that, too."

My jaw drops. That photo went viral and totally ruined Joss's rep.

"She didn't have to do any of those things, though," Liana says. "It was her decision. The same way it was to let me keep believing Swan was alive. That really was unconscionable."

I fill my mouth with burrito.

Liana's gaze drifts out the window. "Swan could be romantic, and sweet. Like, on my birthday I got out of school to find my car stuffed full of balloons. She'd soaped my windows with 'I heart you.'" Liana's lips curl up slightly.

I remember the time, about a week after Swanee and I met, that I found my locker covered with glittery heart stickers. The principal wasn't so happy about her defacing school property. Swanee did help me scrape them all off, though. Then, a few days later, my locker was covered with rainbow stickers.

Liana says, "She'd call late at night and we'd talk for hours and hours. She made me feel like I was the only person in the world. I'd keep trying to hang up, but she'd say, 'Just one more minute.' Which turned into an hour. It was fun, but I was so wasted the next day." Liana stops and lowers her head. "Sorry."

She'd do that with me, too. Tell me how much she loved me and how lucky she was that coincidence had brought us together.

Liana sighs. "We lost our last game on Friday. In OT."

That jolts me back to the present. "Do you like being a cheerleader?"

"Yeah, I do. I'm already planning to try out for the squad at CU. Swan and I were going to get an apartment together in Boulder."

I choke.

"What?"

Now is not the time to tell Liana that Swan signed a letter of intent to go to Arizona State. "I'd like to see you cheer sometime."

"Why?"

"Because I bet you're really good."

She shrugs. "We placed third in Spirit Squad competition this year."

"Wow."

"It's not first."

She's driven, the way Swanee was about her running. "My friend Betheny is a cheerleader. Well, ex-friend."

She picks up on that. "What happened?"

"Guess."

Liana's eyes fix on me. "Swan was definitely the jealous type."

To the point of me sacrificing all my relationships.

"Were you and Betheny...?"

"No. Just friends." Good friends. Best friends.

"Swan was always suspicious of my friends, too." Liana dabs at a smear of sour cream on her mouth with a napkin. "She hated how much time I had to spend with the squad. Like it was one big orgy." She rolls her eyes.

We fall silent again. "Was it?" I say.

She looks at me and, with a mischievous glint in her eye, says, "Yeah. I'd sneak everyone into VS at night and we'd go wild."

I laugh.

She tosses me a lopsided smile. "Tell me about your family."

What's to tell? "My mom's an obstetrician and my dad's an IT consultant. Oh, and I have a baby brother."

"Really?" Her eyes light up. "I love babies."

I want to ask her if the baby I saw in her Facebook album is hers, but she goes on, "I have six nieces and three nephews."

Geez.

"It's the Catholic in us. Big families. Procreation, you know?" Her cell rings. She digs it out of her bag and answers, "*¿Qué pasa?*" She listens as I drain my drink. "Out with a friend." She goes to take a sip. "Dad, I'm still in Denver. Why can't Clarice do it?" She listens and purses her lips at me. I'm drawn to her lips. She has nice lips. Not thin or thick. Just-right lips.

I'm still mesmerized by her lips when she gathers up her trash and mine. "I have to go home. My sister needs a sitter because my mom has her church group and my dad can't even put a bottle in the warmer to heat it up. Thank you again for the ring."

"No problem."

At the door, she turns. "We didn't even get to talk about . . . you know."

Fine by me. It's not her responsibility to reconcile my feelings.

Liana drops me off in front of my house. “So,” she goes.

“So.” That’s it. I feel an unwelcome sense of conclusion as I get out of the car.

I curse myself, curse the world—the underworld, the afterworld—as I watch her drive away.

I’m trapped between two worlds. One is pulling me backward, the other forward. The regressive force is stronger, yet the desire to move on is so fierce I’m having difficulty staying rooted. I know the past is Swanee, but can the future be Liana?

Swanee would be irate if I got together with her. She’d hate both of us.

I know I shouldn’t care, but I do. I have to let Liana go, allow her to move forward so I can.

Chapter 15

Joss is waiting for me at my locker on Monday. She looks... stricken.

"Hi," I say. I realize that Joss was as much a victim of Swanee's actions as Liana and I. Even if Liana's right about our choices being our own, Joss suffered the consequences of going along with Swanee's dares and crazy schemes. "I'm sorry about the car," I say. "And the lock on Swan's door. I hope you got everything out you wanted."

"Who gives a shit about the fucking car? When I get my license I'm buying a Ferrari."

Right. With what money? I should tell her about the cash hidden under Swan's mattress. I assume she doesn't know about it or she would've retrieved it. A few hundred dollars isn't even enough to buy tires for a Ferrari, though.

"The anniversary was last Saturday," Joss says.

All the anniversaries I can think of scroll through my head. No hits. "Of what?"

Joss just looks at me. "She died that day. We missed it."

Oh my God. She did? Time seems to have become a sort of nuisance I have to contend with every day. It's been easier lately, and I should feel guilty about that. But for some reason, I don't.

I spin my combination lock to open the door.

"We should do something," Joss says.

I almost say, Like what? Bake a cake?

Loading up the books for my morning classes, I avoid Joss's eyes. I try to block out the despair she's emanating. It's impossible. "What did you have in mind?"

She doesn't answer. I think Joss needs to talk to somebody to help her with the grief of losing a sister. I say, "You know, we have free grief counseling—"

"Shut up!" she snarls. "No one understands or cares how I feel. Obviously *you* don't." She knocks the books out of my arms and takes off.

I call, "Joss. Come on. I care."

She flips me off.

I guess I deserve that for wanting to forget rather than celebrate. I do care about Joss. I just don't know what to do to help her. I'm not a counselor. Like Mom said, I think her pain is all bottled up, and one of these days it's going to blow up inside her.

Since I can feel my lungs blackening from the secondhand smoke outside, I return to eating in the cafeteria. My choices are alone at a table, reading a book, letting everyone see what a total loser I am, or asking if the GSA will take me back.

I don't even have to ask. A chair magically appears and I sit. The girl to my right says, "Do you want some of my fried chicken?" and the guy across the table goes, "It's finger-lickin' good." Everyone howls. Even I have to laugh. I forgot how great it is to be with this group. "Thanks," I tell her. "I'm not really hungry." At which point everyone at the table begins shoving their leftovers at me. Maybe I am a little hungry. And a little lonely, because I can't remember the last time I heard my own voice joining in the chatter.

I'm doing what I usually do on Friday nights—nothing—when I get a text message from Liana. My heart leaps. It reads:

Fossil Ridge. Saturday at 9

I know I shouldn't jump at her every beck and call the way I did with Swanee. Who is Liana to me? An acquaintance? A friend? Someone who was hidden from me, which adds to the mystery of her.

I'm late for the game because I can't find Fossil Ridge High School. Google Maps sucks. When I finally arrive, the game's already in progress and the bleachers are full. I head for the blue and gold of Greeley West.

The cheerleaders aren't wearing the same uniforms I saw on Liana's Facebook. The skirts are short and pleated, but instead of sweaters the girls are wearing vests. Their spring uniforms? Liana is immediately noticeable, not only because she's in front, but also because she's fantastic. As the squad begins a dance routine that's part hip-hop and part jazz, her movements are sharp and crisp. So cool. She's athletic. Her legs are muscular and taut, like she works out a lot. She's graceful, too. I bet she's taken a lot of dance lessons.

Greeley West scores a run and the cheerleaders all yell and do split jumps in the air. The audience chants the cheers.

I'm not really paying attention to the game, so I'm surprised when people stand and start to leave. Who won? I don't think it was Greeley West, because the players' shoulders are slumped as they head back to the bus, and the Fossil Ridge players are giving one another high fives.

I hang back, watching as the cheerleaders dig out bottles of Gatorade from a cooler. Liana twists open her top and chugs until half the blue liquid is gone. As she lifts the bottle to her mouth again, our eyes meet. I give her a little wave.

As she walks toward me, one of her squad members calls out and Liana says over her shoulder, "I drove in. See you guys tomorrow."

Two cheers lift the cooler and veer toward the school buses, and the parking lot begins to clear.

"You came," she says.

"I didn't think it was a request."

She whaps me on the arm and it sends a tingle up through my neck and head.

Liana doesn't speak until she's dug her keys out of her bag. She turns to me. "Our usual spot?"

"The Chipotle?"

"No, silly. The McDonald's in Broomfield. Is that okay?"

I find my keys. It's more than okay. We have a regular spot.

We order burgers and fries and Cokes, and Liana doesn't even ask me to pay for her combo meal. As we head for the same booth we sat in before, I'm not sure what to say to her. I can think of only one reason she asked me to come today.

"So I guess you want to say a prayer or something for the anniversary. I should tell you that I'm not all that religious."

She gives me a blank look. "What anniversary?"

Is she joking? "You know. Swan's death?"

"What about it?"

"It was a month—well, five weeks ago today."

She unwraps her burger and says, "Not for me. I still have a week to go before the anniversary of the day my life was destroyed."

I cringe. Unwrapping my cheeseburger, I reply, "Is it really that important what day you heard about it?"

"Yes!" she snaps. "Because it changed everything I ever knew about her. Or thought I did. Not to mention that I learned about you."

Well, ditto. My eyes fall and I lose my appetite.

She rakes her hands through her hair and expels a heavy breath. "I'm sorry. There's no reason to take it out on you. You're the only person I can talk to who even halfway understands what I'm going through."

I lift my head and our eyes meet and hold. Not for long, though, because I can't look at her without feeling guilty about the impact of the texts.

"Let's just eat and talk about something, and someone, else," she says. She lifts her burger to her mouth and chomps into it.

She motions to me to eat.

After swallowing, she says, "Our baseball team is the worst in the league, in case you didn't notice. I was almost embarrassed to have you see that."

“I wasn’t really watching the game.” Shit. I should superglue my mouth shut.

She smiles and takes a sip of Coke.

I say, “Tell me about your family.”

She swirls a few fries in catsup. “I have two sisters and three brothers. A mom, a dad, two dogs, three cats, *mi abuelas y abuelos*, but they live in Mexico. My mom and dad are first-generation Americans.”

“Is that why you’re not out to them?”

She frowns slightly. “Who said I’m not out?”

I think back. “I thought you did.”

“No. I finally came out last year. It wasn’t easy. *El que diran*, you know.” She clues in to my oblivious expression and continues, “An unstated law in Latino culture that says you will be judged by your friends and your family for what you do.”

I stick my straw in my Diet Coke. “That must be hard.” I think, Being Catholic can’t help.

She shrugs and bites into her burger again. “It is what it is.”

“Does your family accept you?”

“It took a while. My mom still prays for me. I do think she acknowledges she can’t change me, but she’s afraid of what my life will be like. And, of course, she wants a hundred grandchildren from each of us.”

“You can have children,” I say.

Liana goes, “Try telling my mom that. Just don’t mention turkey basters.”

I laugh.

"That baby in your album on Facebook..."

"Caleb? Talk about *el que diran*. My sister had him when she was fifteen."

My eyes grow wide.

"I know. But we're family, and we love him."

We finish our lunches and talk and laugh about all kinds of things. The only subjects that don't come up again are Swanee and the anniversary. Thank God.

I add Liana to my contacts list on my cell. Not that I expect her to call or anything. But if she invites me to another game, I think I could develop an interest in baseball.

Mrs. Burke hands back our "Ignorance Is Bliss" papers, and I got a D-. At the top she wrote a note: *Alix, of all my students, I thought you'd be the one to figure out that the opposite of "Ignorance Is Bliss" is "Knowledge Is Bliss."*

Shit. I'm so stupid.

Even though I'm intent on listening and taking notes while Mrs. Burke explains our next assignment—writing a critical analysis paper—I can't ignore the buzzing cell in my bag. I take a quick peek at the ID.

It's her.

I know I'm going to need to bring up my grade with this next paper, but I can't stand it. I pull my bag into my lap and read Liana's text:

What are you doing at this very moment?

I glance up to see Mrs. Burke writing on the whiteboard.

I text:

Texting you

LOL. Seriously. Where are you?

English. Meh

She texts:

I love English

You don't have Burke. She should be teaching Middle English. She's that old

Liana texts:

ROFL. Do you get to write poetry?

I text:

God, I hope not

You don't like poetry?

I do. I just can't write it

Have you ever tried?

"I'll take that." Mrs. Burke is hovering over me with her hand out.

Busted. I give her my cell. Not missing a beat, Mrs. Burke continues her lecture, returning to the front of the room, where she drops my cell into her briefcase. It vibrates and a bunch of people snigger and swivel around to *tsk* at me. My face flares.

I try to take notes, but now I'm distracted. Worried Liana will keep calling or think I cut her off. The minutes tick by and I find myself doodling her name: Liana. Liana. Pretty name. It fits her. Liana Torres. It sounds poetic.

The period ends with the blaring of the bell.

"I want to approve your topic and thesis before you begin your critical analysis paper, so write up a paragraph and bring it in on Thursday," Mrs. Burke says as we're gathering our stuff to leave. "You can choose a book, a movie, or anything you feel is worthy of analysis. The subject is wide open. What I'm looking for are your logical analysis skills and writing abilities."

I quickly take down the notes from the board: Purpose (thesis statement); Short Summary; Arguments; Conclusion. I'll have to Google them to find out what each means.

Mrs. Burke is shoving her notes into her briefcase when I stop by her desk. She doesn't glance up.

"Mrs. Burke?"

"Yes, Alix." Still no eye contact.

"May I have my phone back?"

"At the end of the day. I'll be in the English Department office." She heads out the door.

It's *my* phone. She has no right.

As I'm entering the cafeteria, I pass Joss speeding toward the exit. Probably to smoke a joint or six.

I hurry to catch her. "Joss, hey." I put a hand on her shoulder and she wrenches away. "I'm sorry about the anniversary." She doesn't turn around to face me. I'm back at that moment when the RIPs on Swanee's Facebook wall dwindled to zero and I felt livid about what short memories people had of her. "We should've taken a moment of silence or something," I say softly to Joss. "Even if it was just the two of us."

Joss inhales a stuttered breath and her shoulders begin to shake.

"Maybe we can get together and talk—"

"Alix, there you are." Mrs. Burke bustles toward me. "My husband's sick and I have to leave, but I wanted you to have your phone back."

That was nice. I feel bad about assuming she was out to get me personally.

Mrs. Burke says to Joss, "You're going to be late for class."

Joss whirls and I see that black mascara is streaming down her face. "Fuck off," she says to Mrs. Burke.

I cringe.

Mrs. Burke snarls, "That's two hours in detention, young lady."

Fortunately Mrs. Burke pivots and hurries off before she hears the string of curses under Joss's breath. Joss goes out the back while I check my phone.

There are ten texts and a voice mail. I key in my password to listen to the message.

Liana says, "Hi. It's me. Are you okay?"

Immediately, I call her back.

She answers on the first ring.

"My cell got confiscated in class," I tell her.

"Oh, no. I'm sorry."

"It's not your fault. I know the rules."

"So do I. I shouldn't be texting you during the day."

"No. It's fine."

"It's weird, but I feel better talking to you. More hopeful that life goes on. I hope you don't mind," she says.

"I don't mind. I feel the same way." Which is true.

"Where are you now?" she asks. The halls are filling and ears are everywhere, so I slip into the restroom and lock myself in a stall.

"In the bathroom."

"Before class or after?"

"Between. English and lunch."

Liana says, "English. Lunch," like she's writing it down. "I sent a request to friend me again on Facebook. But if you want me to go away and leave you alone, just deny it. I'll understand."

Someone comes in and takes the stall next to me. I have to face the wall and muffle our conversation, which creates a time lapse.

"Okay," Liana says. "Sorry for bothering you."

"No." I lower my voice. "I don't want you to leave me alone. It's just..." I whisper, "Somebody's in here."

"With you? Are you wearing the merry widow?"

I smile to myself. "I wear it every day. Hoping to get lucky, you know?"

She laughs. "Anyway, if you want to talk, I'll need your schedule so I'll know when it's safe to call. And vice versa."

Two things strike me instantly: 1. She plans to call again. 2. Swanee never could remember my schedule, no matter how many times I told her or wrote it down. I knew where she was every second of every day. Or at least I thought I did.

I ask Liana, "Where are *you*?"

"In the locker room, getting ready for a pep rally."

"Why the locker room?"

"So I can pick up my poms and run a brush through my hair. Gotta be glam, you know."

I love her hair. It's thick and curly. I'd give anything to have hair like hers instead of my flyaway mop, which won't even hold a braid.

"Where's your game?" I ask.

"Berthoud."

Before I can verbalize my thought, she preempts it by saying, "Don't come. You've seen us play."

She knows I wouldn't be going to watch their team.

"I'm on in two minutes," she says. "By the way, I took my ring back for a refund? Since I had it sized, they wouldn't give me the total amount, which bites, but I did find out something interesting."

"What?"

"Liana, the band started," I hear in the background.

"I'll tell you later," she says. "You'll die. Sort of the way I did."

Chapter 16

As I veer up the sidewalk, I see that Joss is waiting for me on my front porch. She skipped out on detention, which will only prolong her sentence.

Every time I see her now, I feel guilty that Liana blames her for the texts. She looks like she wants, or needs, to talk. "Would you like to come in? I have Double Stufs."

That was the wrong thing to say.

She brushes past me and clomps off down the walk.

I notice she's gone from goth to slut. She's wearing the shortest jean skirt I've ever seen over holey fishnets with this skimpy, low-cut shirt that shows every bulge. I always think girls who dress like that are crying out, Notice me!

I have this sudden urge to run after her, to hold her, to tell her it's okay to cry, to be angry, to grieve, to scream and curse the world for taking her sister and best friend from her.

Even though I don't know Joss that well, Swanee would

want me to help her through this. I dump my backpack on the porch and dash after Joss.

She's gone. Disappeared. I call out her name and get no response, so I turn back toward my house. Inside, I find Dad in his office with Ethan, rocking him to sleep. Peeking in, I say, "Okay if I borrow the car for a while?"

"Just be back by dinnertime."

I drive in the direction Joss headed, but it's like she vaporized into thin air. I could talk to Jewell, share my concern about Joss needing someone to talk to about Swanee's death. Yeah, right.

As I wonder what to do about Joss, my brain automatically sets Dad's GPS to Berthoud. An hour. Yikes. Being back by dinnertime may be a problem, so I chisel a mental memo to call my parents when I get there so they won't worry.

Liana's right. The final score is fifteen to one, Berthoud. And I only glanced at the scoreboard to make it less obvious how focused I was on Liana during the game. After it's over, as she's slugging down her Gatorade, I come up behind her and go, "Boo."

She jumps and drops her bottle. We both crouch down to retrieve it. She says, "What are you doing here?"

"It was on the way."

"To what?"

"Um, Wyoming?"

We laugh in unison. She says, "We have a better track team. Come to those meets." Her face freezes. "If you can."

We stand there for a minute, not saying anything. My heart starts crashing against my ribs.

"Liana, the bus is leaving in, like, a minute," a cheerleader with brilliant aqua hair says, breaking the spell. "I could use your help with the cooler." She closes the lid.

"You said you found out something when you returned the ring," I say to Liana.

She holds my eyes, and then looks away.

I should've listened and not come. Now I feel I'm being presumptuous.

She swallows hard and her voice goes hollow when she says, "Can we talk about it later?"

She's gone before I can answer.

Shit, shit, shit. I don't get home until after seven, and Mom and Dad are thoroughly pissed. Naturally, I forgot to call. They don't ask where I was, which is a relief, but it also makes me feel like they don't give a damn anymore.

Mom says, "I phoned Jewell to ask if she'd bring over your T-shirt."

"Mom, you had no right!"

"I had every right. I'm your mother. Jewell said she thought you'd already gotten everything you wanted out of Swanee's room." She finishes loading the dishwasher and starts the wash cycle.

I slide into my chair at the table. "I'm sorry. I do have everything. I also figured out they're the most dysfunctional family in the world."

Mom doesn't reply. I think she and Dad figured that out a month ago.

Mom says, "I left you a bratwurst and some sauerkraut in the fridge to warm up."

"Okay. Thanks," I say. "I'm really sorry again about being late and not calling. If you want to take the keys away—"

"Don't give us ideas."

I sit alone at the table with my nuked dinner and think about Liana, whether she lured me to Berthoud with the ring story.

No, that would be more of a Swanee ploy. Liana is nothing like her.

I can't keep placing blame on everyone else. It was my fault for not listening to Liana, my fault for not calling home. We choose our own actions, like Liana said.

Thoughts of my poor choices conjure up the image of Joss. As much as I want to distance myself from the Durbins, I can't seem to erase Joss. Her image, her unresolved grief, my guilt surrounding her.

As if Swanee's taunting me, that night I see the glow of her cell in my bag. I know I should get rid of it. So why can't I? I should give it to Joss, but then she'd know I am the thief and the liar.

I don't know why I'm not ready to relinquish that stupid cell. It's been more than a month, and no doubt the phone is dead or the service canceled. Having it only reminds me of what I've lost.

I can't sleep. I go downstairs to make some hot cocoa and as I pass Dad's office, I see the light on. Mom's in there, working on his computer. She must sense me behind her because she says, "Yes, Alix?"

That sixth sense freaks me out. Maybe I need to change deodorants.

I enter and sit in Dad's "thinking" chair. It's actually where he naps when he thinks no one's looking. "Mind if I ask you a question?"

Mom stops typing and wheels around.

"What would you do if you knew someone was in trouble and you didn't know how to help them?" I ask her.

She says, "Let me guess. Joss?"

Make that a seventh sense.

"Yeah."

Mom says, "Is she on drugs? Because if she is, I think Jewell should know."

What good would that do? Jewell wouldn't care.

"I think she's having sex with a guy who's, like, twice her age. But that's not the problem."

"That's not the problem?"

"Mom, please. Okay, it's a problem. But it's not the worst problem."

"What could be worse?"

"No one's talked to her about Swanee's death."

Mom says, "I'm sure Jewell and Asher have."

I'm sure they haven't. "I think she needs professional help. Like, grief counseling."

Mom holds my eyes for a long time, and then picks up the phone. She must know a slew of psychologists and counselors. When the call is answered, she says, "Is this Joss?"

Oh my God.

Mom asks, "Is either of your parents home? This is Dr. Van Pelt. Alix's mom?" She listens a minute. "Will you leave a message for Jewell to call me—" Mom holds the phone away from her ear. Slowly, she hangs up. "Does she always talk to people that way?"

"Pretty much."

"I'll keep trying to get hold of Jewell or Asher. You did the right thing in telling me. That girl needs serious help." Mom reaches over and pats my knee.

"What are you going to say to them?"

"I'm going to tell them exactly what you told me."

"Leave out the sex part. And don't tell them it came from me."

Mom says, "I'm not leaving out anything."

"Mom, I don't have any proof she's sleeping with that guy. I'm more concerned about how she's dealing. Or not dealing. And keep me out of it when you talk to Jewell, okay? Which I know sounds selfish..."

Why did I even start this conversation?

Mom nods. "I'll do my best."

My brain says get up and go, but my body doesn't respond. Mom starts typing again. She stops and glances over her shoulder. "Is there something else?" She sounds busy and I know I should leave so she can work.

"How do you do it?" I ask.

"Do what?"

"Deal with sick babies. Watch them die, knowing there's nothing you can do to save them."

Mom swivels around in the chair again. Her face softens. "Did I ever tell you why I wanted to become an obstetrician?"

I shake my head.

"I was in college, changing from one major to another. The ten-year plan, you know?" She smiles a little. "I just didn't feel passionate about anything. Then I took this urban studies class, and half our grade was doing community service. There was a list of places where we could volunteer and I chose a safe house for women and children. This one young woman, about my age, showed up on my first day of work. Yasmin. She was eight months pregnant. She also had twin boys who were three or four. We got to be good friends. She was funny and smart and ambitious. Unfortunately, her boyfriend was your typical abuser. Jealous and full of rage. He had to monitor and control Yasmin's every move. And when he drank or did drugs..." Mom shakes her head.

"So anyway, one day I was at the shelter cleaning, and a friend of Yasmin's brought her in. She'd been beaten severely, and by the time we called the ambulance, she was going into labor. Before the EMTs arrived, the baby started coming. The EMTs were trying to save Yasmin and the twins were acting up and the staff was trying to calm them. I guess I was in the right place at the right time because I was the one who caught the baby. It was like a miracle, Alix. This little life in my hands. Yasmin couldn't speak, and I'm not even sure she heard me tell her, 'It's a girl.' She died on the way to the hospital."

"Oh my God," I gasp.

"But her baby lived. It's the one you save, the one you can, that gives the work meaning and purpose." Mom meets my eyes. "I hope you find that in your life."

I stand and head for the door.

"Alix?"

I stop and turn.

"You're not responsible for Joss."

So why do I feel I am? I may have lost a girlfriend, but I can't even imagine how it must feel to lose your sister and best friend.

Chapter 17

As I'm Googling all the parts of a critical analysis paper, my cell rings. It's Liana.

"What are you doing?" she asks.

"Looking online for a critical analysis paper to plagiarize."

When she doesn't laugh, I say, "Kidding."

"I knew that."

I think we're still kind of feeling each other out, knowing when we're serious and when we're joking around. Liana says, "She never made one payment on the ring."

It takes me a moment to process the remark.

"I don't know when, but she took it off layaway and got her money back. Obviously, she never intended to give the ring to me."

Was that the cash under her mattress? If so, it was a lot. "How much did she put down? Do you know?"

"A hundred, that I saw. She said she was making payments every week."

More lies.

Liana adds, "I found out when I went to return my ring and saw that the matching one was back on display."

Oh, God. That had to hurt. I can't think of anything to say except, "I'm sorry."

Liana goes, "Whatever. I just want to get past it all."

Me too, I think. I'm getting rid of that cell, the sooner the better.

"So what are you doing?" Liana asks. "Besides committing a felony?"

"Is it?"

"I don't know. Plagiarism may only be a misdemeanor. Either way, you're going to do hard time, girl. I was wondering..." Her voice trails off.

"What?"

"If. Maybe. We could meet again?"

My heart pounds in my chest. "Sure. When? Where?" Do I sound too eager? "Our regular spot?"

"Yeah. Friday our game's in Broomfield, at four. It should be over by five thirty."

I'll have to get permission from Mom and Dad to miss dinner. "I'll try," I tell her.

She says, "If it's a problem..."

"No. No problem. My mom and dad just think we should all eat dinner together."

"Yeah, we have that tradition, too. It's hard, though, when everyone has work and sports. But I like it when we can all be together."

Maybe I should appreciate our family traditions, too. Except in this case. "I'll be there," I say.

* * *

The next morning, just as I'm going to ask about Friday night, Mom says, "I wasn't going to go to the annual obstetrics conference in Dallas this weekend, but there's a special session devoted to new developments in prenatal care, and I'd like to attend. Your dad's college roommate lives in Fort Worth, and he hasn't seen him in years, so he'd like to go with me."

What? No, please, no. "You can't leave me alone with Ethan."

"It'll only be Friday and Saturday nights."

"I can't. I have plans on Friday."

"Cancel them," Dad says from his spot at the stove.

Odds are everything will be fine, but I can still feel the terror of Ethan almost choking to death the last time I babysat. And why Friday?

"We'll leave after you get home from school and be back by Sunday afternoon," Mom says.

She must see the panic on my face because she adds, "It's only two nights."

Forty-eight hours of impending doom for Ethan. And eardrum damage for me.

"Can't you ask Jennifer?" I say.

"We're asking you," Dad replies. "It's time you took more responsibility for Ethan. He *is* your brother."

"I feed him, don't I?" And I've changed about a gazillion diapers.

Dad sets a plate of buttermilk pancakes with blueberries and whipped cream on top in front of me. Sheer bribery.

"You'll be fine," Mom says. "And I'm sorry about your plans. You'll just have to reschedule."

Dad adds, "No wild parties while we're gone."

Like I have enough friends to invite to a party.

On my way to school, I text Liana:

Friday's out. My parents are going to Texas and I have to babysit

She texts back a few minutes later:

What's in Texas?

Cattle?

Moo

And BBQ

She texts:

Yum ☺

We carry on silly convos for the rest of the week. She's crazy fun to talk to. She makes me laugh. She makes me wish I was meeting her Friday night.

I ask Mrs. Burke if I can have an extension on my critical analysis paragraph, since I have nothing to turn in on Thursday. "I have a subject in mind"—a minor fib—"but I want to make sure there's enough there for a thesis, evidence, and conclusion." Hopefully that'll show her I've been thinking about it, at least.

She narrows her eyes, and then says, "Okay. But Monday at the latest."

By Monday I may be incarcerated for plagiarism, child abuse, or both.

Friday I take the long route home, thinking, If I'm late

maybe Mom and Dad will cancel their trip. Yeah, right. The long route means passing Swanee's cul-de-sac, and I see that the Smart car is gone. I know I should feel something—like the final link to Swanee has been broken. I don't feel anything, though. Except maybe sad for Joss.

Awesome idea to walk the long way. It's starting to rain, or sleet, and I'm soaked by the time I get home. Mom's standing in the hallway with her rolling luggage, and Dad's behind her holding Ethan in his carrier. Mom says, "I've left you Jennifer's number, in case you need anything. But please try not to bother her. Our hotel info and itinerary are on the fridge. Ethan has a bit of a runny nose, so I've written down his pediatrician's number, too. You have my cell, and your dad's."

And 911.

Dad hands Ethan off to me and immediately a bolt of anxiety shoots through me. Two whole days? Ethan must sense my fear because he lets out a whimper. Dad smooths his hair and says, "You'll be fine, buddy. Your big sissy has thought of all kinds of ways to entertain you. Right?" He looks to me for confirmation.

Like leaving choking hazards around, I don't say.

"Have a good time." I trudge after them to the door and into the garage.

Dad shoves his and Mom's suitcases in the back of Mom's SUV and says to me, "Alix, I don't know if I feel comfortable with you driving Ethan around. But if you have to..."

"I won't," I say. I'll be watching his every move.

We stand there as if in suspended animation until Dad says, "We better hit the road, Jack."

Mom gives me a brief hug. Dad looks like he might hug me, but then changes his mind. They both get in Mom's SUV and back out of the driveway.

Ethan starts to cry. Inside, I unstrap him, pick him up, and try to quiet him. He screams louder. "Ethan, please." He's screeching and fighting me so hard I'm afraid I'll drop him. I cross to the living room and try to sit him in his swing. He kicks and kicks. What's wrong? It's like he associates me with danger, the way he should.

"Ethan, come on. You like to swing. See?" I push his swing back and forth.

He screeches like a crow. Tears spring to my eyes because I don't know what to do. I set Ethan in his playpen and find one of his toys, the plastic keys on the key ring. Could he swallow those? I toss them away and find a stuffed koala. He slaps it away. There's a pacifier on the coffee table, but I'd have to take my eyes off him to reach it.

I lift him again and he arches his back away from me. He's strong and struggling.

"Please, Ethan. Give me a break."

Maybe a bottle. I take him with me to warm a bottle. It feels like I have a death grip on him, hard enough to squeeze the air right out of his lungs. What if I drop him, though? What if he breaks a bone or dies from head trauma?

I set the bottle in the warmer and turn it on.

Ethan is bawling and kicking, clenching his fists, and I don't know what to do. Just as I'm about to call Mom or Dad and admit I'm a total failure as a sister, the doorbell rings.

"Ethan, chill," I say to him, but he pounds on me all the way to the door. I don't even check the peephole; I just fling it open.

It's Liana.

"Hi." She smiles. All I can do is stare at her.

"Our game was rained out." Her smile fades. "Is that your brother?" She has to raise her voice to be heard.

"Yeah. Ethan."

"What's the matter with him?" He stops wriggling enough for me to open the screen door and let her in.

"He hates me."

She makes a face. "Babies can't hate. Can I help?"

"I'd kiss you if you could."

She presses her arm into mine. "Promise?"

A tingle prickles my skin.

She takes off her wet parka, hangs it on the doorknob, and takes Ethan from me. "*No llores bebé, todo va a estar bien*," she says. Rubbing his back, she coos, "*Ya ya ya.*" It's like a miracle. He instantly stops crying. She nuzzles her face into his neck and I see all his muscles relax.

"How did you do that?" I ask. "What did you say to him? Whatever it was, teach me."

She moves around the living room, stroking Ethan's head and murmuring in his ear in Spanish. "He feels hot."

"He has a runny nose. And he had a bug not too long ago. Do you think he's sick? Should we call the doctor?"

She feels his armpit. "How long has he been crying?"

I glance at the clock on the microwave. "About twenty minutes." Is that all? "Time flies when you're going deaf."

Liana smiles at me. "It could be he's just upset. Could you bring me a cool washcloth?"

While I'm in the kitchen wetting a washcloth, she calls from the living room, "He's adorable. He has your nose."

When did she notice my nose?

"And your gorgeous green eyes."

My cheeks are burning as I hand her the washcloth. She's the one with the gorgeous eyes. She sets Ethan on the sofa and bends forward, tickling his belly. He grins.

He does have my eye color. I always thought my eyes were this unremarkable hazel, but on Ethan, they glow like jade.

I sit on the sofa arm, watching her gently dab his cheeks and forehead. She starts to make a game of it, dangling the washcloth and making him reach for it.

He giggles.

She's good with him. A natural. No wonder she loves babies. "God, I'm glad you came. He might've screamed for hours with me. Then the neighbors would've called Child Protective Services to remove him from an abusive situation."

She says, "Don't be silly. He would've calmed down."

"You don't know him. He really does hate me. Plus, he's afraid I'll hurt him."

She casts me an odd look. I tell her about the button incident, and she says, "It was an accident. Babies stick everything in their mouth. Caleb swallowed a penny once, and it took him two weeks to poop it out."

"Ew. Who had to look for it?"

"There are some things only a mother can do."

I look at her and we both laugh. She grows serious and

says, "About what I told you before. *El que diran*? I don't want you to get the wrong idea. Family always comes first, and we all embrace and care about one another." Liana stands up and hands the washcloth to me. "You play with him now."

Reluctantly, I take the washcloth. "He'll start screaming." We trade places and I get a whiff of Liana's hair or body gel. Whatever it is, I can't stop inhaling. She's wearing her uniform, and I see goose bumps on her legs. "If you're cold, you can turn on the fireplace," I say. "The remote's on the coffee table."

She presses the On button while I bop the washcloth up and down. Every few bops I let Ethan grab it. But as soon as he puts it in his mouth, I pull up. Still, he's grinning.

Liana moves to the fireplace and rubs her arms. Her skin is so smooth and brown, and there's more than heat from the flames warming up the room. I ask, "Do you want a sweatshirt or something?"

"No, I'll be good in a minute."

"Thank you," I say to her.

She turns around and gazes into my eyes. "For what?"

"Saving my life. And Ethan's."

Liana's gaze stretches on and on. It's like neither of us wants to be the first to break it off. At last, Liana returns to the sofa, bends down, and presses her palm against Ethan's forehead. She says, "He's much cooler. I think he's fine."

I want to say, I think you're fine. Better than fine.

Ethan lets out a little sigh. I touch the tip of his nose and he rewards me with a smile.

Liana trickles her fingertips through his feathery hair. "He really is precious."

He is, actually.

Liana says, "Do you have something to drink?"

I jump up. "Yeah, of course." Where are my manners?

I reach down to lift Ethan but stop because I know he'll cry if I pick him up. His eyes hold steadily to mine and I don't detect a hint of terror. I give it a try and he actually grasps my neck with his little hand.

Liana follows us to the kitchen, slowing to peer out the window into the yard. "I love your house," she says. "Just the feel of it. There was something about Swan's that was... I don't know. Cold. Or twisted. Chaotic clutter."

And I always thought the clutter was cozy. Homey.

"Sorry to bring her up. Let's not ever talk about her again."

"Deal." I feel relieved. Elated. Liberated.

Balancing Ethan on my hip, I check the fridge. Mom must've stocked up before she left. "We have Sprite and Diet Coke. If you're hungry, I could make homemade pizza."

"That sounds fantastic. As long as I get out of here by eight thirty or nine."

"It won't take that long." I hand Ethan to her and pull out all the ingredients for a pepperoni, sausage, and three-cheese pizza.

"Sprite for me," she says.

I lug out the bottle and then retrieve two glasses from the cupboard. As I set her glass in front of her, I see Ethan standing on Liana's lap at the table, playing with her earrings.

My breath catches. "Where did you get those?"

"What?"

"The earrings." The ebony button ones I made for Swanee. "Never mind. I know where."

Liana removes Ethan's hand from the earring. "She said until she could pay off the ring, she hoped these earrings would do."

"I bet she said she made them, too."

Liana doesn't answer.

I almost feel like crying. Then I feel like throwing the measuring cup against the wall. "I made them. For *her.*" If I look at Liana, I'll lose it.

"I'll give them all back, Alix."

"Forget it. They were a gift. She had the right to do whatever she wanted with them."

For a long minute Liana doesn't speak. Then she says quietly, "When do the lies end?"

I close my eyes. Apparently not with death.

Chapter 18

The phone rings and Mom tells me they arrived. Already? I check the clock and it's almost nine. Time soars when you're eating pizza with a beautiful girl, while your baby brother is safely tucked away in his carrier, sound asleep. Mom asks how things are going and I say, "Great."

"Did you have a hard time putting Ethan down?" she asks.

"Not at all. I've been mainlining him with Robitussin."

"Alix."

I don't want to tell her he's not upstairs in bed yet, since I'm afraid to leave him alone. "We had a good time. He was actually kind of fun." I hear her tell Dad what I said as I smile at Liana.

Liana checks her watch and freaks out. Hustling to the living room, she makes a call on her cell.

Mom says, "If you need anything, you have our numbers."

I'm not going to call because I'm determined to prove to them that I'm responsible and trustworthy. That I am a good sister.

"Your mom?" Liana asks as we both end our calls.

"Yeah. Checking up on me, which was actually a good idea, since you saw what a stellar babysitter I am."

Liana gives me a little push on the shoulder. "You're doing awesome."

"Yeah. Once you showed up."

She says, "I have to go."

"Will you help me put him to bed first?"

She follows me upstairs. As we transfer him to his crib, he whines, but Liana rubs his arm until he calms and his eyelids flutter. I bend down to kiss his forehead. He smells sweet, like baby powder. I've always loved that smell.

As I hover over him, Liana whispers, "Are you going to stay here all night?"

"I thought I would."

"Alix, he'll be fine. You have a baby monitor. Just turn it on and keep the other one with you."

Baby monitor. "Hang on." I pad into Mom and Dad's room to retrieve it. I hope my maternal or paternal instincts are as sensitive as Mom's or Dad's if Ethan wakes up and cries. Or coughs. Or chokes.

Liana heads downstairs with me on her heels. She puts on her parka.

"I can't thank you enough," I say.

"Thank you for dinner. It was awesome. You're now my personal chef."

"At your service," I say with a bow.

The conversation stalls. "Well?" she says.

Well what? Her dark eyes seem to bore right through me. "You promised."

Oh my God. Does she mean . . . ? My throat is dry and I lick my lips. She does the same, and then takes a step toward me, leans in, and touches her lips to mine. The explosive sensation that travels through me is like a volcanic eruption. How long the kiss goes on is anyone's guess. Eventually one of us breaks it off, and I swear it's not her. She opens the door and slips out before I can even exhale the breath that's seized my lungs.

I must've fallen asleep with the baby monitor to my ear because when I wake up I have a rectangular groove on my cheek. No sounds are coming from the speaker and I think, He's dead. He rolled over and suffocated. I race to his room and find him in his crib, playing with his toes. When he sees me, he starts to bounce and smile. So cute, except he smells like a diarrhea factory.

As I change his diaper, I realize I didn't give him a bath before putting him down last night. He's still got some gunk in his hair from dinner. I decide to feed him breakfast first, so I can wash off all the layers at once.

Ethan's a splasher and soaks my entire front. When I shampoo his hair, I give him curly ringlets, then a faux-hawk. We could do this all day, except the phone rings downstairs. I know better than to leave him alone, even if it is a safety tub.

As I'm toweling Ethan dry, the phone rings again, so I wrap the towel around him and lug him downstairs with me.

"Hi," Dad says. "How're things going?"

"Good." Except we broke our bath routine, which will probably scar Ethan for life.

"What do you have planned today?" he asks.

"I don't know. I thought we'd sharpen all the knives."

Dad chuckles.

"Do you want to say hi to Ethan?" I stick the phone to Ethan's ear and hear Dad talk to him. Ethan's eyes widen and he says something resembling "da-da." If he's ever said that before, I'm not aware of it.

I take the phone back. Dad asks me, "Did he just say what I thought he did?"

"I think so. Do you think he's a savant?"

Dad laughs. "He might just have gas."

We talk for a couple more minutes, until Ethan gets squirmy. "I should let you go," I tell him. "SpongeBob awaits."

As soon as I hang up, the doorbell rings. Who could be coming over? I peer through the peephole, but it's black, like there's a hand over it. "Who is it?" I ask.

No answer.

What if it's a kidnapper? Someone who's been casing the house, waiting for the right moment? I've been watching too many cop shows. Still...

I open the door just a crack and my jaw drops.

"Hi," Liana says.

I open the door all the way and unlock the screen. "What are you doing here?"

She pouts. "Do you want me to leave?"

"No." God, no. She enters and a blast of cold air blows in with her. I notice it's still drizzling.

"Rained out again?" I ask.

"No. About half the players are sick with flu, so the coach forfeited the game. Sucks. But it'd be miserable cheering in this weather." I take her coat from her and she reaches for Ethan. "He's naked," she says.

"We just took a bath and I haven't had time to dress him yet."

"Or yourself."

I scan my front and see that all I'm wearing is a sleep shirt, and it's plastered to my body with bathwater. Everything is visible. I hug myself.

"Can I dress him?" she asks.

"Absolutely." I start to sprint up the stairs, and then stop and let her pass. She doesn't need to see my old jockeys.

I could take a shower, since she's watching Ethan. Instead I pull on a pair of sweats and a T-shirt. When I come out, she's still in Ethan's room.

"He has the cutest clothes," she goes. She chose these oversize denim overalls with a red-and-white shirt and red high tops.

"When they're not covered with baby crud."

She lifts him into the air and he squeals with delight.

"How long can you stay?" I ask. Please say all day and night.

"Until you get sick of me." She rolls up the cuffs of the overalls.

I smile at her. "Then I hope you brought your toothbrush."

She returns my smile, her eyes teasing.

Even standing this close makes my heart pound. "What do you want to do? Dad doesn't want me to take Ethan anywhere, so we're kind of limited."

"We don't have to do anything. We could watch a movie."

A movie. Please don't be into Johnny Depp. "That sounds good."

As we head toward the stairs, Liana says, "Is this your room?" She stops at the threshold.

"Yeah."

"Can I see it?"

God, did I leave unmentionables strewn about?

She hands Ethan off to me before wandering in and checking out my stuff. My laptop, iPad, books, dolls and stuffed animals from my childhood. For some reason, I want her to approve. She points at the rainbow sticker I have on my dresser mirror. "Did you get this at Pride?"

"No. Rainbow Alley."

"I've never been there. I'd like to go."

"I'll take you," I say.

"When?"

"Whenever you want."

Her phone rings and she digs it out of her back pocket. She speaks in Spanish to whoever's on the line. "I don't know." She eyes me. "Three o'clock?"

I hold up five fingers, twice, like, Make it ten o'clock.

She grins. "I'll be home before dark, okay? *Te amo.*" She ends the call.

Crouching down, she picks up the rainbow earring out of my tackle box, which I haven't yet put away.

"Wow, this is cool. I do plan to give you all your earrings back."

"Like I said, you don't have to."

"I didn't mean to upset you."

"Why would it upset me? Who cares if the only thing I ever made for her didn't mean shit?" This pique of anger rises inside me and my eyes well with tears. DAMN. DAMN HER. I go over, latch the tackle box, and kick it under the bed.

Liana walks up behind me and rests her head on the back of mine. Ethan's little hand clutches my ear gently. A tear escapes and slithers down my cheek. I wipe my nose. She turns me around and holds me.

I can feel her breath on my neck and it makes me shiver. We lean back and gaze into each other's eyes, and all I can think is, I want to kiss you so badly.

But she steps away and says, "Where's your Kleenex? In the bathroom?"

I nod. She goes in and comes out with a few tissues and hands them to me.

I blow my nose. She gives me space, circling the rest of my room.

Ethan gets squirmy and I say, "I think I forgot to give him his bottle. Meet you downstairs."

I warm a bottle, relieved to have put some distance between Liana and me. She sets off every nerve ending in my entire body. I curl on the sofa with Ethan and his bottle, while Liana sits on the other side, as far away as possible. Thank God.

"Want me to check the On Demand movies?"

"Sure," I say.

She scrolls through and there's nothing we want to see. It's all I can do to keep Liana out of my peripheral vision.

She spies Dad's *Little Miss Sunshine* DVD and says, "I *love* that movie."

"I do, too." Although I'd never admit it to Dad.

She inserts the DVD. I place Ethan in his playpen and pull it over in front of us so he can watch, too.

About ten minutes into the movie, she fluffs an accent pillow under her head and lies down, kicking off her shoes and stretching her legs across my lap. "Okay?" she asks.

Ethan's drifting off, sucking a pacifier, so I pull her legs closer to me in answer, and then tickle the undersides of her feet. She yelps and kicks. I whisper, "Quiet. You'll wake him up." We get into a leg wrestling match. Then, I don't know how it happens, but we're kissing. She's on top and I'm holding back her hair and she's pressing her body into mine. She raises her head and looks at me, and she must see the desire and need I'm feeling because she resumes. Only she shifts and rolls off the sofa. I reach out to stop her fall, but plop on top of her. She giggles and takes me in her arms.

Ethan whimpers and we both halt the action to check on him. Sound asleep.

"We shouldn't be doing this," she says softly.

"Don't worry about it. If he wakes up, I have plenty of bottles in the fridge."

She clicks her tongue. "I don't mean that."

"Oh." But I want to. And no one's here to stop me. I kiss Liana. The kiss stretches on and I feel that hitch in my lower belly.

She breaks off the kiss and says, "Do you think this is some kind of revenge thing?"

"I don't know, and I don't care."

She smiles. She kisses me again. Her lips are so soft, and my need is so great. My hands have a mind of their own and begin to roam up her sides and down her legs. We're lying side by side and my hand sneaks up between her thighs.

She pushes me away a little. "Don't."

The same thing I used to say to Swanee every time we got this far.

Eyes lowered, she goes, "I'm still a virgin."

"What? No way. In six months, you never . . . ?"

"I won't lie to you. I wanted to. But you couldn't move an elbow in that stupid Smart car, and she wanted to do it in my car, which I thought was gross. I told her I'd split the cost of a hotel room, as long as it wasn't infested with roaches and bedbugs."

I laugh. Sort of hysterically. It startles Ethan awake and he starts to cry.

Crap. Liana pushes to her feet and lifts him out of the playpen. "He's wet."

"I'll get a diaper," I say.

I run upstairs with wings on my feet. They never did it. I don't know why it makes a difference, except it's one thing Swanee wanted and never got. From either of us.

* * *

After Liana leaves, I know exactly what I'm going to do my critical analysis paper on. Hopefully, Mrs. Burke has seen the movie and understands its contribution to the role of humor in bolstering the spirit of humanity.

I finish my outline, then lie in bed and replay what happened today. Did I make the first move? Did Liana? Does she want me as much as I want her? And is it for revenge, like she said?

I should feel guilty and ashamed about falling for her, especially since Swan's been dead for such a short time. But wasn't she the one who said how lucky we were that coincidence brought us together?

The baby monitor echoes a muffled wailing from Ethan's room. I run in there and find him turned over onto his stomach, trying to roll back. Resettling him, I hum and rub his arm the way Liana did, but it doesn't get him back to sleep, so I pick him up and take him downstairs. In the living room, I put him in his baby swing and tug it over in front of the TV. I don't guess it matters what he watches or when, but who knows how early in life you're damaged by all the sex and violence on TV? I remote around until I find *South Park*, which is sort of a cartoon. Right?

The phone rings and I feel my heart leap, thinking it's her.

Dad says, "I hope I didn't wake you up. Just checking in."

Checking up is more like it. And of course Liana wouldn't call on our home phone. I reassure Dad that all the knives were sharpened with no bloodshed.

He says, "We'll be home in the morning, but we switched to an earlier flight."

Why? What if Liana comes again? "Stay another night if you want," I tell him. "Stay two nights."

"We could never do that. We miss you too much."

Is he serious? It's only been a day and a half. You'd think they'd want to get away more often. I can't even remember the last vacation they took alone.

Out of nowhere, he goes, "We're really proud of you, Alix."

For finally being the sister I always should've been? A lump forms in my throat.

"Alix?"

"Ethan just woke up. I better see if he needs a bottle or something." I mumble a quick good-bye. Ethan's glued to the TV and I think, Great. Now I've planted the seed for a couch potato.

As if he read my mind, he whines like he's hungry. I warm a bottle and cradle him in my arms on the sofa, singing softly as he suckles. The first song that comes to mind is "Born This Way," by Lady Gaga. He seems to like it because he grins and claps his hands. I wonder what Liana's doing now. If she's attracted to me as much as I am to her. What'll happen next, if anything?

I should call or text her. Ask point-blank.

I'm so sure. Like middle school: *Do you like me?*

Ethan's bottle rolls off my foot and I blink back to the present. He's sound asleep. I turn off the TV and gingerly lift him up, draping him over my shoulder without a towel. If he spits up, all this milky goo will run down my back.

I don't even care.

My cell chirps upstairs and I want so badly to take two stairs at a time, but I know it would jar Ethan awake.

After I tuck him in and kiss him, I tiptoe to my room.

A text message from her:

I'm sorry if I went too far today

I text back:

No. I am

It takes her a long time to reply and I think the conversation's over. Another text arrives:

We need to stop apologizing. It was the same with she-who-shall-not-be-named. I was always apologizing for something, always feeling bad or inadequate

I text immediately:

Me too!

All these memories come surging back. She hated my clothes; she told me I should lose weight, exercise more. She didn't like my taste in music and movies. She resented the fact that I had to eat dinner with my family, and spend weekends doing chores or homework. Any time I wasn't available was like a personal affront.

Liana texts:

She'd show up at my school and expect me to just take off. I couldn't do that. I had cheerleading, and a job. Then she'd accuse me of not loving her enough

I text:

That sounds familiar

Except unlike Liana, I did give up my life for her. I gave up everything.

Liana texts:

How's it going with Ethan?

Good. Great. He woke up and I got him back to sleep. You wove some kind of magical spell on him and now he loves me

She texts:

He's always loved you

I read that line again and realize I've always loved him. And I'll always have his back.

I had fun today, she texts. I always have fun with you

Me too

Que tengas dulces sueños. That means sleep well

U 2. That means you too

LOL

After we disconnect, I lie there and gaze up into the dark, feeling slightly intoxicated. Something—a flickering light—bounces off the ceiling. It's Swanee's cell in my bag. The glow-in-the-dark decal on the case is starting to fade. A final memory sears my brain. Something she said a few days before I decided I was ready. We were in her car, parked behind Safeway, and I almost, almost let her go all the way. When I pushed her off at the last second, she said, "For fuck's sake, Alix. I've never met anyone who hasn't had sex by the time they were seventeen."

Liar liar liar.

I straggle out of bed, kick the bag with the cell into my closet, and shut the door.

Chapter 19

Mom and Dad walk in around noon, as Ethan's finishing up breakfast/lunch. There's baby cereal splattered all over Ethan and me, the table, and the walls. I was hoping to have a chance to swab the deck before they got home.

Ethan squeals and reaches up for Mom. She takes him, giving him belly spuds. He giggles his head off.

I say, "I know it's a mess—"

"You done good, kiddo," Dad cuts in. "Thanks for stepping up." He gives me a little squeeze around the shoulders.

Actual physical contact. I begin rinsing out a sponge at the sink to wipe down the walls.

"Don't worry about this." Mom waves me off. She tells Ethan, "Say *ma-ma*."

Dad murmurs in my ear, "I told her Ethan said *da-da* first and now she's jealous as hell."

Whoa. My parents rarely curse.

I leave the sponge on the counter and ask, "Can I go out for a while?"

Mom says, "Sure. And thank you again, Alix."

I can't grab my hoodie from the front closet fast enough.

At the first stop sign, I text Liana:

We're on

She texts back:

YAY ☺. Meet at our regular?

I beat her to the McDonald's. The smell is too tempting, so I begin to slam down my cheeseburger deluxe and fries before she arrives. I ordered her favorite combo, and as she scoots into the booth, she says, "Ooh, I could kiss you."

Do it, I think.

Our eyes meet and the electricity sends a shock wave through my body. She inhales a ginormous bite of burger and garbles, "What do you want to do today?"

"I don't know. Have sex in your car?"

She snorts and kicks me under the table. "There's this event in Boulder where you go around to a bunch of artists' studios and watch them work. Does that sound like good times?"

"It sounds awesome."

"It's free, too."

She pulls out a brochure and we pore over it. There are potters and painters and glassblowers. A map of all the studios is included. We decide to take my car, but Liana doesn't feel comfortable leaving hers in the parking lot at McDonald's, so she asks if I'll follow her home.

As we drive through Greeley, I note it's kind of a juxtaposition of farming community/cow town and cool college campus. The University of Northern Colorado is spread between plots of land with buildings of diverse architectural styles. Students are out playing Frisbee or walking to or from dorms.

When Liana swerves to a curb, I pull in behind her. She locks her car door and heads back to me. "Come meet my family," she says.

I glance at her house. It's a two-story redbrick bungalow. The kind of house I'd like to own someday.

"If my mom starts praying on her rosary beads, just make the sign of the cross and say, 'And with your spirit. Amen.' "

Is she kidding? I practice to myself as we head up the walk. She opens the door and an older man greets us. "Papá," Liana says. "This is Alix."

"Hello, Alix." He extends his hand. "Liana's told us everything about you."

I widen my eyes at Liana. Like what?

She smacks his arm. "Stop it."

His hand is so large it envelops mine. "Nice to meet you," I say.

"Let me go grab a jacket in case it gets chilly," Liana says, leaving me alone with her father.

He says, "Sit," indicating a well-worn sofa. I sink into it. He plops into a leather recliner across from me, leans back, and folds his hands over his middle. He has thick curly hair that's going gray at the temples, and a mustache. "Tell me about yourself."

I gulp. What does he want to know?

"How do you know Liana?" he asks.

"Um, we're just friends."

He smiles as if he reads more into that than I intended. Or not.

I add, "I don't go to her school."

"No?" He arches his bushy eyebrows. "Where do you go?"

"Arvada," I say.

"That's a long way from here."

"My parents just got back from Texas." Wait. Did he ask about them? Have I answered all of his questions?

"So they travel a lot?"

"Hardly ever."

Liana returns. "Okay, I'm ready."

Thank God, I think. Another minute and I'd be volunteering my life story.

We walk back to my car and Liana says, "Did he ask you if we were sleeping together?"

"What?"

She laughs. "You should've told him you were on the Pill and not to worry."

The artists run the gamut. Boulder's known to be eclectic by nature, and a lot of the artists look like they stepped out of a time machine from the hippie era. But they all have one thing in common: their passion for their work.

As Liana and I stand and watch a glassblower create a delicate vase, I can feel the artist's joy at creating something from nothing. All of her pieces are twisted twice at the neck, which must be her trademark look.

My gaze drifts to a shelf where a collection of glass swans are displayed. My lunch threatens to reappear. I see Liana looking, too, and she says, "Let's get out of here."

We visit about six pottery studios, where I'm amazed at how a glob of clay can be thrown on a potter's wheel and shaped into a perfect bowl or plate or cup.

This one artist uses recycled junk to make centerpieces and candle sconces. They're original and beautiful.

The last studio on our list is a jeweler. It's within walking distance, and without even thinking about it, Liana and I intertwine our fingers. She smiles and says, "Are you having a good time?"

"The best," I reply.

Her fingers tighten.

A bell over the door to the jeweler's studio tinkles when we enter. Four jewelers share the space. One makes silver-and-turquoise earrings, bracelets, and rings. They're gorgeous, but too conventional for me. The jewelry that really captures my attention is in a glass display case. All the pieces are copper. The jeweler behind the counter sits at a wooden table, pounding out copper he's cut into geometric shapes to blowtorch together in layers. "Hi," he says to me. "If there's anything you want, it's all on sale."

"Thanks." Even the sale prices would set my Visa limit back two months.

He asks me, "Where did you get your earrings? I've never seen anything like them."

Liana twists her arm through mine and says, "She made them herself."

He gives me a nod of approval. "If you ever want to rent out studio space here, let me know."

Is he serious? No way does my caliber of work compare to these professionals'.

Outside the studio, Liana says, "You want me to ask him how much it costs for a space?"

"No. It's only a hobby. I'm not that good."

She makes a face at me. "You underestimate yourself. I bet you could make a living at your art."

No one's ever called it art. We head back to my car and Liana asks, "What are you planning to do after you graduate?"

I've been avoiding thinking about it. "I don't know. Be a nanny?" At that moment, my cell rings. The sound of my parents reminding me I'm nowhere near old enough to make my own life decisions.

It's Dad. "Where are you?" he asks.

"In Boulder."

"Boulder! Doing what?"

I almost say, Practicing free love. "Taking this tour of artists' studios."

"Are you alone?"

I gesture to Liana, like, Poke a stick in my eye.

She laughs.

"No," I tell him.

"Are you with Betheny?"

"No."

"Is it okay to ask who you are with?"

Why does it matter to him? "I'm with my friend Liana." Becoming more than a friend.

Dad asks, "Will you be home for dinner?"

I have to be, don't I? I check my watch and it's after three. That should be plenty of time. "Yeah."

"You can ask your friend to come, too, if you want."

I don't think I'm ready to thrust Liana into the Van Pelt pit.

Liana and I continue to the car and I unlock the doors with the key fob. I expect her to get in, but instead she snakes her arms around my waist, pulls me to her, and kisses me. I feel my bag clunk to the ground and my knees go weak. We might've stayed like that for hours if someone hadn't driven up next to us and honked.

We both climb into the Prius, look at each other, and laugh.

A crazy, out-of-nowhere laugh.

That night Liana texts me:

Best. Day. Ever

I text back:

What's better than best?

We text for a while, until I hear Mom's beeper go off. It's after midnight and I know she must be exhausted.

Liana texts:

Thanks for accepting my friend request

It reminds me that I need to send her my class schedule.

I text:

School night. You better get your dulces sueños in

LOL. U 2

A few more texts and we hang up.

I grab my laptop to send Liana my schedule. I want hers, too, including work and extracurricular. I notice my relationship status still says In a Relationship, but Swanee's name is gone. When I look for her in my friends, she's disappeared. Someone took down her page. Which is just as well. I change my relationship status to Single.

Then I have this wild idea. She'll probably say no, or ignore it, but I send a request to Liana asking her to confirm that she and I are in a relationship. A second later, a response comes in. I give a little squeal of joy. She accepted.

When I hand in my critical analysis outline to Mrs. Burke, she seems impressed. It's so much more than a single paragraph. Of course, if she doesn't approve of the topic, I'm back to square one. A smile curls the corners of her mouth and she says, "I love this movie."

Score!

The paper isn't due for a while, but I bet if I hunker down I can finish it in two or three nights. I know the grade on my persuasive paper is on my permanent record, but an A on this one might boost my average to a C+ or B-.

Liana spends practically every day cheering at baseball games or track meets. We still talk or text during the day or at night, but I miss being with her, physically. Long-distance relationships suck.

At dinner on Thursday Dad says, "Earth to Alix."

Who says that anymore?

"Does that sound okay to you?"

"What?" I say.

He turns to Mom, "Do you think we should get her hearing checked?"

Mom holds up three fingers and raises her voice at me. "How many fingers do you see?"

"Eleven," I say. "My hearing, and vision, are fine."

Dad says, "I was asking how you would feel about spending spring break up in Vail. One of my clients has a timeshare condo he won't be using and he asked if we'd like to rent it."

Visions of snowboarding for a week perk me up. "That'd be awesome. All of us?" I ask.

Mom answers, "Of course."

"What are you guys going to do?" Neither of them skis anymore, and Ethan's too little. Unless they expect me to babysit while they rent snowmobiles, in which case we might as well stay home.

"We'll stay busy," Dad says. "We can go tubing or sledding. I think there are horse-drawn carriages. Ethan will like that. You and your mom can go shopping."

When was the last time Mom and I shopped together? In elementary school, shopping for new clothes.

Mom adds, "We could take a side trip to Glenwood Springs for the day. Soak in the hot pool. That sounds idyllic to me."

It sounds like heaven.

I didn't even realize spring break was next week. It snuck up on me.

"Well?" Dad says.

"Well... yeeeeah."

"I'm on call Saturday, so we'll leave Sunday," Mom says. The phone rings and she gets up to answer it.

I hear Mom say, "It's for you, Alix."

Who'd be calling me on our home phone? I answer and it's Joss. "Stay the fuck out of my life!" she screams. "You have no idea what's going on, and anyway it's none of your fucking business!"

I cringe. Mom must've talked to Jewell.

"For your information, Swan took me to Planned Parenthood for birth control months ago. I'm not a moron."

"I never said you were."

"Swan's the only one who got me," Joss says in this croaky voice.

That may be true, but I care. I want to ask her if she's in counseling yet, if Jewell is doing anything to help.

Joss snarls, "The fucking bitch stole Swanee's iPad from my room."

Why do you need it? You have memories, I want to say, but that would only set off another rant.

"Do you have any pictures?" Joss asks. "I want all the pictures of her that everybody has. She was *my* sister, and they belong to me."

Pictures. I do have the pictures from Swan's cell that I uploaded to my PC. I could transfer them to a flash drive and delete them from my machine. That would remove every trace of her from my life. Except the cell.

Is that what I want? I know it's what I need.

"I know you have pictures on your cell," Joss says.

I blink back to the moment. "Yeah, I do. I could put them on a flash drive, and you could get prints."

Joss stalls. "I can't afford to make prints. Could you do it?"

Still forcing me to pay. I should say no, but I can't find it in my heart. "Sure."

"Okay." She lets out a calming breath and then adds, "For your information, my boyfriend—the only guy who ever liked me for myself—dumped me." She disconnects.

Chapter 20

When I tell Liana we're going to Vail over spring break, she says, "The whole time?" I can hear the disappointment in her voice.

"But we can still talk. And I promise we'll get together as soon as I'm back."

"When you get back, it's my spring break. My dad always takes a group of students to archaeological sites or on digs, and I go with him. Last year we went to Machu Picchu, and this year we're doing a dig at the field school in North Park, near Walden."

"Pond?"

She snorts. "No, silly. Walden, Colorado. Population five. It's close to Steamboat Springs."

"Will you have a chance to ski?"

"I wish. Mostly I help lug equipment and record Dad's lectures."

"Woot," I say unenthusiastically.

"It's cool. I really like going."

"Are you thinking about becoming an archaeologist?" I ask.

"No," she replies. "I plan a double major in Mexican-American studies and poli-sci."

If only her ambition would rub off on me.

She sighs. "I wish I was coming to Vail with you."

"That'd be a blast. Sext me, okay?"

"Ha! Only if you sext me first."

I can't imagine either one of us sexting.

"I wish we could see each other at least one more time before you leave. You know how you asked if I like being a cheerleader? Sometimes it sucks."

Totally. "Break a leg," I tell her.

"Don't say that! I fell off the pyramid my sophomore year and broke my wrist."

Yikes. "Don't break anything. I want you whole."

"I want you whole, too," she says softly.

This trickle of warmth seeps through my bones.

On Saturday, Dad asks if I'd mind going to the store to pick up diapers and formula. Since Walmart is on the way, I grab the flash drive to make prints for Joss. Naturally, today of all days, their photo machine is down. I ask if I can leave the flash drive so that they'll have the prints ready when I get home.

Liana calls me while I'm upstairs packing. "Do you think we could Skype while you're gone?"

Duh. "Why weren't we Skyping all this time?"

"Because it'd make me want to be with you even more than I already do. I hate being apart."

"Me too."

"But let's do it anyway."

We exchange Skype names and talk for a while. Before we end the call, Liana says, "You're getting under my skin, Alix Van Pelt. I can see why she-who-shall-not-be-named fell so hard and fast for you."

"Ditto, Liana Torres."

We talk for another hour or two or three and I forget all about packing.

The people who don't go to Mexico for fun in the sun on spring break swarm to the Colorado ski resorts. The slopes are overrun with skiers and snowboarders. As I'm riding up the lift with two college students—a guy with his arm looped around a girl's shoulder—I wish so badly that Liana were here with me.

It's awesome having a condo right in the heart of Vail. I can actually walk from the building to the ski lift. There's a balcony on every unit, and as I'm nearing the bottom of the hill I think I glimpse Mom and Dad, searching for me. I wave, and then do a face plant. That should impress them.

Around lunchtime I get hungry, so I trek back to make a sandwich and see if Mom and Dad are there. They aren't, so I check in the fridge for something, anything, to eat.

People must have been using the time-share, because there's a fairly fresh loaf of bread, along with peanut butter and blackberry jam. I make a sandwich and then go out on the deck to eat and to watch the skiers. The weather is sunny—a cloudless, sapphire sky. Sitting with my feet up on the railing, I call Liana, figuring she should be home from church.

She answers on the first ring. "I hope you're on the lift. Because I think it's a felony to snowboard while using a cell phone."

Maybe she should major in law. "I'm taking a break. Laying—or is it lying?—in the lap of luxury," I tell her.

She says, "I hate you." I know she's kidding. "I wish I was laying—or is it lying?—with you."

"It's kind of lonely," I tell her the truth. "Do we have time to Skype?"

"Sadly, no. I have to leave for work in five minutes."

"No fair peeking in the dressing rooms," I say.

She goes, "You're such a buzzkill."

I smile. We talk until she says, "Eek. I'm late. And my cell is almost dead." Mine's drained, too, so I head inside to recharge it. Mom's coming in the door with armloads of groceries, and I relieve her of the bags. "Where are Dad and Ethan?" I ask.

"Schlepping around town," she says.

I help her unload the groceries and put them away.

"I bought all this food, and now I don't feel like cooking," Mom says. "Want to go out or have something delivered?"

The sandwich only whetted my appetite. "Definitely," I say. "Let's go out."

She sits at the condo's dinette and opens a folder with a bunch of menus in it for all the restaurants in town. "It's nice to see you happy again," Mom says. "We've been worried about you, you know."

I don't meet her eyes. "What did you expect?"

"I'm not talking about Swanee dying. Of course you'd be upset about that, but every day you were with her, you were... drifting."

Drifting. What does she mean? I guess I know. How Swanee was trying to make me into someone I wasn't. Manipulating me. Making me feel inadequate, the way Liana said. Not only that, but pulling me away from my parents.

They do need to realize that at some point they'll have to let me go, and vice versa.

"Haven't you ever felt like you've made sacrifices for Dad?" I ask. "Done things you didn't really want to do?"

Mom seems to consider the question. "I suppose I've adapted. We both have. But we've never asked each other to sacrifice who we are as individuals. And if we really had a moral objection to something the other wanted, we would've talked it out and compromised. We've given, not taken away. We've grown stronger together."

The same way I'm beginning to feel about Liana. When she's not with me, a part of me is missing.

"What about Chipotle?" Mom says. "There's one right down the street."

Chipotle. I have to smile. *"Mucho bueno."*

After lunch and two more hours of boarding, I'm totally wiped. We all go out for a nice meal at an Italian bistro and I almost fall asleep at the table. When we get back to the condo, I tell Mom and Dad I'm going to bed.

Snuggling under the covers, I fluff up two pillows and log on to my laptop. Before I Skype Liana, I should text her to see if this is a good time. My cell's in the kitchen, still charging, so I have to get out of bed to retrieve it. Mom, Dad, and Ethan are in the living room with the lights off and soft music playing.

"Sorry." I unplug my cell. "Forgot this."

"Who are you calling?" Mom asks.

"Um, a friend."

"Do you have to?"

"I'll be quiet. Promise." I don't wait for Mom's response.

In my room I text Liana:

Can you Skype now?

She doesn't text back. I sit with my laptop until the screensaver kicks in. I must doze off because the Skype sound on my computer jolts me awake.

It's her, Skyping. I press Accept.

"Are you there, Alix?" she asks. "Can you hear me?"

"Yeah. Let me just..." Her face comes into view and my heart jumps.

"I can't see you," she says. "Let me check my video...." After a second, my face appears on the monitor.

"There." She smiles. "We're connected."

We are, I think. In more ways than one.

"Tell me about your day," she says. "Minute by minute."

"The snow was perfect, and it was warm. Lots of people, though."

It's almost as if she's here with me. Except I can't touch her, or smell her, or feel her body heat.

A knock sounds on the door. Mom sticks her head in and says, "We're going to bed."

"Okay."

Liana says, "Who's that?"

Shit. "My mom."

Mom glances at the computer. "Who are you talking to?"

"Liana," I tell her.

"Let me say hello to your mom," Liana says. I make a face at her, and she reciprocates.

I turn the laptop toward Mom. She perches on the bed and I adjust the monitor until Mom's face is in the video section.

"Hi," Liana says. "I just wanted to tell you I think Ethan is the cutest baby in the world. Aside from my nephew, because I can't be prejudiced." She grins.

"Thank you." Mom blinks at me, and then looks back to Liana. "When did you see Ethan?"

"That time you and your husband were out of town—" Liana stops. She must realize I never told Mom I had company, or she sees something in Mom's face, because she adds hastily, "I just stopped by for a little while to visit Alix. I didn't even know Ethan would be there."

Mom's lips draw taut.

Liana says, "I better get to my homework. I'll talk to you later, Alix." By the time I swivel the laptop back around, Liana's hung up the Skype phone.

I expect Mom to lay into me for letting strangers in the house, especially when she and Dad aren't there and it's only Ethan and me, but all she does is say, "Your dad was right. She's pretty. Does she go to Arvada?"

"No." That's as much as I'm willing to give up for now.

"Invite her over when we get back—"

"Her break starts that day, and she's leaving for a dig with her dad and some archaeology students." I shut the lid on my laptop. "But I will."

A gleam infuses Mom's eyes.

"What?" I say.

"Nothing." She bends down and kisses my forehead. "See you in the morning."

Chapter 21

The day I get home Liana doesn't text or Skype, so I figure she's on her way to Walden. I leave her a voice mail to call or text as soon as she can.

On Tuesday morning she texts me right after my alarm goes off.

Can you Skype? I only have a few minutes until Dad comes back to get me

God, I have bed head and my teeth feel fuzzy. We link up and, naturally, she looks like she just stepped off the pages of *Elle*. "Where's your dad?" I ask.

"Scouting the location. It's pretty desolate here. Nothing like Peru. But on the way up, we saw three moose. Hang on. I'll send you a picture."

When it arrives, I marvel at how enormous they are. I've seen lots of elk, but never a moose.

"Dad splurged on the lodging, so we're staying at the Hoover Roundup Motel. Yee-haw. I have to share a room, so there's not much privacy."

All I can do is look at her and project myself across the miles.

She says, "Wish you were here," at the same time I say, "Wish I was there." We laugh.

We talk for a while until Mom calls up the stairs, "Alix, you're going to be late."

Liana says, "I don't know if I'll be able to Skype every day, but I'll try to get some time away from the group in the morning or at night to call you. Okay?"

I'll take every precious moment.

We linger, like we want to say something else to each other. Liana puts two fingers to her lips and sends me a cyber kiss before the Skype call ends.

On my way out the door, Mom hands me a bunch of brochures. "For Joss," she says. "Of course, you can read them, too. I hope you know your dad and I are always here to talk to."

I glance at the titles: "The Five Stages of Grief," "How to Handle the Death of a Family Member," "Dealing with the Loss of a Loved One." I think I've dealt pretty well, thanks to Liana.

Joss is waiting for me at my locker before lunch. Shit. I forgot to pick up the pictures. Liana's on the phone, saying, "The week I come back I either have to cheer or work every day, but I have an invitational in Denver on Saturday. It should be over by five."

I hold up a finger to Joss. "I'm coming for sure," I tell Liana. "Where is it?"

"Jeffco. We could go to dinner afterward. Then maybe get a room?"

My heart thumps in my chest. Is she . . . ?

"Kidding."

I don't know if I feel relieved or bummed. If she was serious, there wouldn't be anything holding me back.

While I'm twisting my combination lock, Liana says, "I'm counting down the days."

I say, "I'm counting down the seconds. Tick, tick, tick..."

She laughs.

I love how her laugh stimulates all my senses.

Joss is staring daggers at me, so I say, "Can I call you back?"

"I need to get out to the dig, anyway. Talk to you soon."

We disconnect.

Joss says, "Who was that?"

"Just a friend. Your prints should be ready. I'll stop by after school and pick them up. Okay?"

"Swan's ashes aren't even cold," Joss says stonily.

She must've cued in on the tone of my voice when I said "a friend." Or maybe the whole conversation gave us away.

"I brought these, in case they might help." I fish through my pack for the brochures Mom gave me.

Joss skims the titles and says, "Do they say, 'Replace a dead person with someone new as soon as possible'?"

She has this knack for making me feel guilty and diminished. The way Swanee did.

Joss throws the brochures practically in my face and stalks off.

When I drive up to my house, Joss is sitting on the porch stoop. To apologize? Hard to imagine, but anything's possible.

She follows the Prius into the garage. I'm not even out of the car before she says, "Did you get them?"

The pictures. "Yeah."

She holds out her hand. I shut the door and pass her the package. It's a thick envelope and Joss asks, "Do you want to look through them with me?"

If I say no, will that sound cold? If I say yes... I close my eyes and this unexpected veil of sorrow drops over me. Will I ever get over her?

Joss isn't even wearing a coat, and she has on that skimpy skirt with no leggings. "Let's go inside," I tell her. "I'll make us some hot chocolate."

She just stands there with a blank expression on her face.

I'm not going to wait for an answer because I'm freezing.

Fortunately, she follows me in.

Dad's in his office working. He's set up Ethan's swing near his desk and the rocking has lulled Ethan to sleep. Dad steps out of the room and stretches. "How was school?"

"Torture, as usual," I answer for both Joss and me.

"Good. Our tax dollars at work."

Joss actually cracks a smile.

"Don't encourage him."

He pours a fresh cup of coffee while I nuke two cups of cocoa with marshmallows.

"How are you, Joss?" Dad asks her, casting her that pity-party look.

I think, Please don't go off on him. Please please please.

Joss mumbles something incoherent. Thank God.

I motion to her with my chin to the living room and Dad

returns to his office, closing the door. Remoting on the fireplace, I kick off my shoes and curl my legs under me to get comfy.

Joss holds the package of photos in front of her like it's the Holy Grail. All I want is to get through them and then go back to my happy place. She removes the first picture and stares at it for a year. Finally she passes it to me. Swan and Joss, in a close-up head shot, cheek to cheek. Memories come crashing down a mountain and I feel smothered by rubble. I have to set down my hot chocolate because my hands start to shake.

Joss is still examining the second picture. If we have to go through each one this slowly, we'll be here all night.

"Could we speed it up, Joss? You can spend more time with them at home."

She twists her head to face me. "I thought you'd like to take your time."

"I do, but... I have them on my computer. Remember?"

Joss blinks. That seems to appease her. What she doesn't know is that I deleted the pics as soon as I uploaded them to the flash drive. To fill the time between pictures, I ask, "What do you have against Hispanics?"

She looks at me. "Nothing. Who told you I did?"

I almost tell her it was Liana but stop myself in time. Swanee lied to Liana about that, too, creating this toxic relationship between Joss and Liana. Why? What purpose did that serve?

Joss pulls out the next picture and gasps.

"What is it?" I lean over and Joss wrenches the picture

away. It flies out of her hand and lands faceup on the floor. Before she can grab it, I catch a glimpse. It's the one where Joss exposed herself.

Joss shoves the photo into the envelope and goes to the next one.

"I'm not sure how that got on my cell, but I'll delete it for sure."

Joss swallows hard. "Swan told me the band dude would definitely notice me if I sexted him. I wrote that guy that it was for his eyes only, and Swan told me to add, 'Come and get it.' Then he sent it to everyone, and the cops showed up at our house."

Oh my God. "I'm so sorry, Joss. Some of the stuff Swanee did really hurt and humiliated people. Including you."

Joss snaps, "She didn't mean to."

Really? I go to snake an arm around Joss's shoulders but get a definite vibe to stay back. I add, "She didn't think through a lot of her pranks, and what the negative effects on people might be."

Joss sits for a long minute, her shoulders slumped. I sense a crack in her veneer and say, "Do you want to talk about it?"

She shrugs. "They were jokes. She liked to fuck with people's heads. It was hilarious."

"I'm not laughing."

Joss goes to make a wisecrack and then stops herself.

"Do you want to talk about her death?"

Her head swivels and her eyes go cold. "No. She's gone. Sayonara."

"Joss—"

She takes all the pictures back from me and slides them into the envelope. Pushing to her feet, she walks out without another word, shutting the door behind her.

I'm mad all over again. Furious. Seething. "Way to go, Swanee."

During my Skype call with Liana I recount everything that happened today, adding, "And Joss doesn't hold any prejudice against Hispanics. I don't know why Swan told you that."

Liana says, "I take back every mean thing I ever said about Joss. Except she had no right to text me after Swan's death. That was a cruel prank."

"Yeah, about that..."

Mom raps softly on the door and opens it a crack. She's holding Ethan. Instinctively, I twist the monitor away so Mom can't see who I'm talking to.

She says, "I need to run to the hospital and your dad's at a meeting. Can you watch Ethan?" He's examining a plastic rattle like it's some mystery of the universe.

"Sure," I say.

She hands him over. Saved by the bro.

"*Hola, chiquito,*" Liana goes. She wiggles her fingers at him.

Mom leans down. "Hi, Liana. How are you?"

"Fine, thank you, Dr. Van Pelt. And you?"

"Stork days are almost always good ones." Mom smiles.

That would've sounded insane if I hadn't told Liana my mom was an obstetrician.

Ethan plants his gooey hand on my monitor, smearing Liana's features.

"Your dad should be home in an hour or so," Mom says to me.

"No hurry."

She leaves and I balance Ethan between my legs in front of my laptop. Liana says, "I've been thinking about where we should go after the meet next Saturday. Besides Motel 6."

"Damn," I say. "And I already made a reservation."

She grins. "I'd really like to go to Rainbow Alley. If you wouldn't mind."

"That'd be cool. They might have a drag show, or karaoke. I'll check the schedule."

She says, "Please don't make me do karaoke. I'm so bad."

"You mean I finally found your weakness?"

She laughs. "I have a gazillion weaknesses. I just don't want you to see them."

"Why not?"

"Because I want you to think I'm perfect in every way. Ha!"

"Now my life's goal is to find out everything you suck at."

"It's a long list," she says.

I doubt that.

Ethan flails his rattle and bops me in the face. It makes Liana giggle, and then we're both giggling. It's like Mom said; she makes me feel like I could adapt—in a good way. Become more giving, complete, with someone willing to grow with me, and vice versa.

* * *

I don't see Joss the rest of the week. I figure she's ditching, still going through the pictures. Fixating on them, like they're the only memories of her sister. I wish I could find a way to make Joss open up to me. Or to someone. I know you can't help a person who doesn't want help, but at what point do you give up trying? If it were me, I'd hope at least someone cared enough to never give up.

Friday, on my way home, I drop a sealed letter in the Durbins' mailbox addressed to Joss. Hopefully, Jewell won't open it. All I wrote is, *I'm here whenever you're ready to talk. XO Alix*

Liana and I have been calling and Skyping every day, and when Saturday finally arrives I feel as hyper as a kid at Christmas. I ask Dad at breakfast if he'll drop me off at Jeffco Stadium.

"What's going on at the stadium?" Dad asks.

"A track invitational."

He's almost finished cleaning up from Ethan's breakfast. "Mind if we go along? Your mom's working, and it'd be nice to get out of the house."

"Um, sure." That wasn't exactly the plan. But he wouldn't intrude on Liana's and my plans. Would he?

He adds, "If it's an all-day meet, I'm not sure either one of us would last. A little fresh air wouldn't hurt, though."

He read my mind.

When we arrive at the stadium, Dad heads straight for the Arvada section, but I stop. I search the parking lot and don't see Liana's car. "Are you coming?" Dad says, stepping up the bleachers. Across the track, the Spartan cheerleaders are carting their cooler, and Liana emerges from the pack. My stomach jumps. She shields her eyes, gazing across the track and up into bleachers. Looking for me, I know. As if a magnetic force pulls us together, our eyes meet. She sprints toward us and I call up to Dad, "I'll be back in a minute."

We haven't seen each other in person for weeks. Liana's not even guarded about hugging me, lifting me off my feet, and twirling me around. She's strong. I know we both want to kiss, and it's maddening that we feel the social pressure of not being able to.

"I was wondering if you were just a dream." She holds me at arm's length.

"All real."

She holds me tight again and the world fades away. Then the announcer breaks through our bliss and Liana takes my hands. "Is there somewhere I can change after the meet? I don't want to wear my cheerleading outfit to dinner and Rainbow Alley."

"But there's a drag show. You'll fit right in."

She shoves my shoulder playfully.

"You can change at my house," I tell her.

"Good. Are you going to sit with Arvada or GW?"

I glance up into the stands. "My dad's here, so I guess I have to sit with Arvada."

"Where is he?" She follows my gaze up the stands, and then waves.

Dad waves back.

"Catch you after the meet." Liana squeezes my hand, sending a shock wave through my body.

I clomp up the bleachers and plop next to Dad.

"Where does Liana go to school?" he asks.

"Greeley West."

"Holy moly. That's a drive."

"Tell me about it."

He says, "Do you want to sit over there?"

"Could we?"

He smiles. Then he gets up and heads down the bleachers with Ethan in tow, and we circle the track. Liana greets us with a beaming smile and my knees go weak.

The meet starts with the boys' events. The 100 and 300 meters. My concentration is solely on Liana. She's gotten more beautiful, more talented. I've missed her like crazy.

Dad turns to me and says, "Do you ever think about her?"

I *am* thinking about her.

"Okay, that's a dumb question. Of course you do. But I wonder if Liana isn't a rebound. Have you considered that?"

What is he...? Oh, Swanee. I'd be lying if I said she doesn't cross my mind. But what Liana and I have is real. It has nothing to do with Swanee, and everything to do with us. Liana and I never talked about a rebound relationship—only one based on revenge. Are they the same? I don't think so.

I could only commit to one person, unlike Swanee, who seemingly was able to switch her love on and off like a faucet.

When I don't answer, Dad says, "Never mind. It's your life. You have to learn these things on your own. I just don't want you to get hurt."

She's not a rebound. She may have been there when I needed her most, but that doesn't make her a rebound. Does it?

Arvada wins the high jump and across the track our pep squad goes wild. My eyes stray to Betheny, doing split jumps and rustling her poms. She's an awesome cheerleader, too. I wonder if I ever told her that. Now, of course, I'll never get the chance.

Dad rubs his lower back and says, "I think that's about it for us." Ethan's getting fussy for a bottle. "Are you going to call me when you're ready to leave?"

"Liana and I are going to dinner, and then Rainbow Alley. She's driving."

"How late will you be, do you think?"

"Not very. Rainbow Alley closes at nine."

He squeezes my shoulder on the way down. As he's retracing his steps around the track, I see Betheny jog over to say hi to him. She swoons over Ethan. It's been months since she's seen him, so he must look gigantic.

I should've followed Dad, since I need to use the restroom and it's by the concession stands on the other side. I want to tell Liana I'll be back, but she's conferring with the squad. People are gathered around the bleachers near the concessions, eating and smoking. Joss is there.

"Hey, Joss," I call to her.

She looks gaunt and pale. Grounding her cigarette in the dirt, she starts toward me.

"I need to..." I point to the restroom. "Be right back. Don't go anywhere."

When I come out, she's gone. Then I see her over by the track. "Hi." I come up beside her. "How are you?"

"Fuckin' awesome."

"Did you get my letter?"

"I got it."

Silence. Then, out of nowhere, she says, "I was here when she died."

"What? Where?"

"Here. At the track. She wanted me to time her, like I always did."

My jaw unhinges. "You were here?"

She blinks at me. "Do you have a problem with earwax? She liked running on this track, since it'd give her an advantage at the state meet." Joss returns her gaze to the field. "We climbed the fence. It was still dark, so the cops wouldn't see her on the track. No one would. I'm the one who called 911."

Wait a minute. "The story I got was that she was gone before anyone found her."

Joss continues, "It was cold that day. I brought a thermos of coffee for me and a bottle of water for Swan. She did her stretching, then started running. She was in the zone. You know how she gets."

Got, I think. "Then what?"

Joss stares into the middle distance. "I set the coffee down to find her stopwatch, and when I looked up, she was already on the opposite side of the track. On the ground. At first I thought she was just resting, so I yelled at her, 'You're losing time by sleeping, slacker.'" Joss's voice goes hollow. "She didn't move. So I called louder. I got up and walked across the field, thinking she was just faking it, and when I got there, she wasn't breathing. I knew she had her cell because she always carried it, so I called 911, and they told me how to give her CPR." She adds, "Pronounced dead on arrival."

Oh my God. "Joss," I say. "I'm sure there's nothing you could've done. According to Mom, most people who have sudden cardiac arrests die instantly. Their heart just stops. CPR wouldn't have brought her back." Didn't Mom say that? I think Joss needs to be released from the guilt. I touch her shoulder and say, "You can't blame yourself."

She stares at my hand, and then up at me. "I don't." From her pocket she removes half a joint and lights up. She inhales deeply, closing her eyes. If Joss was here…if she witnessed everything…that makes it ten times worse.

"Could you loan me a couple of dollars for a hot dog?" she says. "I'm starving."

All I have is a twenty, which I was going to use to split dinner with Liana. I hand the bill to Joss and tell her, "Keep the change." I'll charge dinner.

She stuffs it in her back pocket and heads off. The concessions are swarmed. It must be lunchtime.

Suddenly, my eyes are covered from behind. "Three guesses," Liana says softly in my ear. "And the first four don't count."

I smile and pivot. She takes both my hands again and I lean into her. Our attention is diverted by someone beside us, and the smell of mustard.

It's Joss, back already.

"You remember Joss," I say to Liana.

"I do," she says. "Alix explained everything to me, but I have a question. Why did you text me on Swan's cell after she was dead?"

Joss curls a lip. "I don't know what the fuck you're talking about."

I should confess. I need to. But not in front of Joss.

Joss slit-eyes both of us. Her eyes travel to our linked hands and back. "I hate you," she snarls. "I hate both of you."

Chapter 22

When the meet is finished and the parking lot begins to clear, Liana's at her car, waiting for me. I trot over and we embrace, and then she kisses me so passionately, I feel I'm sinking into quicksand.

A couple of guys whistle at us, reminding me that the whole world isn't ready to accept love for love's sake. "Do you remember how to get to my house?" I ask Liana as we climb into her car.

"You're permanently plugged into my GPS," she says.

That gives me a thrill.

I tell her about Joss being at the stadium the day Swan died. Giving her CPR. Hearing the EMT pronounce Swan DOA.

A look of shock, and then one of dismay, crosses Liana's eyes. "No one should have to go through that, especially your own sister." She reaches over, takes my hand, and pulls it into her lap.

Every time she touches me, it's like a beehive of activity all over my body.

Liana says, "I'll light a votive candle for Joss to get through this."

Which is sweet, but I'm not sure it'll be enough.

When we get to my house, I tell Liana to park at the curb rather than in the driveway, just in case Mom's home and has to take off for an emergency.

She's already at the hospital. Dad's in the kitchen and comes out to greet us. "How'd your team do?" he asks Liana.

"So-so. The girls won more events than the boys."

Dad cuts a look at me and I remain impassive.

"We're just going to change before we go out," I tell him. I veer toward the stairs with Liana trailing behind.

Dad clears his throat.

Oh, for God's sake. "I'll wait here." I roll my eyes as I pass her on the way down.

She takes her pink Victoria's Secret carryall into my bedroom and closes the door.

"When and where did you two meet?" Dad asks. The timer dings on the bottle warmer and Dad moves back to the kitchen to lift Ethan out of his high chair.

"It's kind of a long story." It's also awkward standing here, waiting for Liana to return.

Dad cradles Ethan and begins to feed him. "I have time."

"No, you don't. It truly is an epic saga." One that will forever remain untold.

Thankfully, Liana's a quick-change artist and emerges from my room. She looks awesome in everything, but tonight she's wearing black jeans with an eyelet blouse.

My shredded jeans and sloppy tee will never do. I hate to leave Liana alone with Dad, but I tell her, "I'll be fast."

When I come down, Liana's got Ethan in her arms and she and Dad are laughing. She's so great—comfortable with everyone, and self-confident. Two things I'm not.

Dad gives me the requisite blah-blah: Don't pick up strangers. Don't drink and drive. You know your curfew. For no reason at all, he asks, "Do you need any money?"

I had money until I gave it to Joss.

Liana says, "Tonight's on me."

What? It's the first time anyone's taken me out on a date—and paid for it. I feel . . . special.

Once we're in the car, Liana says, "Put on this blindfold. I want to surprise you."

Uh-oh, I think. I'm not big on surprises. When I hesitate, she says, "I wouldn't do anything to hurt or embarrass you."

I know that. The blindfold is a bandanna that smells like her. I tie it tight in back. "If we have to go too far, I'll get carsick," I warn her.

"It's not that far away," she says. "Unless I get lost."

We drive about ten minutes, and then Liana makes a sharp turn and parks. "Okay, you can take off the blindfold."

I pull it down and look at our surroundings. I meet her eyes. "Are you insane?"

"I'll probably have to go to confession, but what the hell?"

We both start to giggle. I've always wanted to come here, but I've never had the guts.

Naturally, it's filled with guys. Big-screen TVs are blasting different sporting events. The hostess says, "Hi. Welcome to Hooters. Two for dinner?"

I can't help staring at her boobs. They have to be fake, or

enhanced. No doubt she's wearing a push-up Victoria's Secret bra. Liana glances sideways at me as we're led to a table, both of us suppressing laughter.

The menu is extensive. Hooterstizers, burgers, hot wings, salads. My attention wanders and Liana pokes me. "Eyes on the menu."

Every waitress in this place is totally stacked and gorgeous. I know I should be a hard-ass about objectifying women, but hey, when you've got it, flaunt it. Right?

We both build our own burgers and share an order of curly fries. It's hard to talk with all the noise from the TVs and guys, well, hooting. But it doesn't matter. We share a chocolate shake and gaze into each other's eyes. Who needs to talk?

When the bill arrives, Liana snatches it up.

"Are you sure you don't want me to pay half?" I ask her.

She reaches across the booth with her empty hand and weaves her fingers through mine. "I'm taking my girl to dinner."

This ember of joy sparks a blazing fire inside me. Does she consider me her girlfriend? Nothing in the world would make me happier.

Outside, as she's unlocking her car door, I step in front of her. Taking her in my arms, I kiss her, and then whisper in her ear, "I love you."

She smiles tenderly into my eyes. "I love you, too." She kisses me until I can barely breathe.

On the drive to Rainbow Alley, I ask Liana, "Do you think we're both rebounding? You know, from she-who-shall-not-be-named?"

Liana takes a long moment to answer. "I know it happens to people because they have this empty space in their hearts. But I never felt the kind of love for her that I do for you. It's like I finally know what real love is."

Her words infiltrate my soul and I know exactly how she feels. What I had with Swanee seemed like love, but now I wonder if it was just infatuation. My need to fill my empty place.

A sense of liberation comes over me, like I'm finally free of her. Whatever hold Swanee had on me is gone. Knowing what I know about her now, I can definitely say I'm glad it ended. Not the how, but the when.

"Where are you?" Liana asks.

"Here." I smile at her. "With you."

Rainbow Alley is downstairs at the LGBTQI Center in Denver. Dance music hits us as we descend the stairs. "What are these?" Liana asks, pointing to the tiles on the wall. Each is made of fired clay and expresses some aspect of the emotional journey toward coming out, or living your truth: fear, courage, compassion, support, acceptance, love, etc. That's what I tell her. She stands at the wall to read a few of them, encircling my waist with her arms. We've shared this journey, even if it wasn't together.

Liana's never seen a drag show, so I know this'll be cool for her. The furniture is pushed against the walls, making room for the entertainment. From the snack table, we fill a plate with pretzels, chips, candy, veggies, and dip before finding a cozy corner on a sofa to snuggle up together.

She gazes into my eyes and I communicate back with

mine. Then she sticks a jelly worm halfway into her mouth and baits me to bite off the other end.

The drag show starts and people whoop and cheer. Tonight is retro: Madonna and Cher. We finish our food and I set the plate on a table beside me. As if on cue, our faces close the distance and we kiss. It's a gentle kiss, sweet, with a little salt mixed in from the chips. We kiss again and my yearning unleashes itself. She shifts so that we can hold each other closer. This time I feel passion and desire in her kiss.

It's as if we're floating up and away from reality and everything that's kept us apart. We're one. We were always meant to find each other, and now it's finally come to be.

"I never thought I'd trust anyone again," she says, stroking my hair. "But I trust you, Alix, with all my heart and soul."

Hearing these words, I feel like I hit a concrete wall. I have to tell her about the texts, my deception. We can't begin this relationship with a lie.

She holds my face between her velvety hands and kisses me deeply, putting her whole self into it.

I'm physically sick. Pulling back, I say, "I need to use the restroom." As I'm untangling from her, my foot catches on the strap of my pack and the contents scatter.

Liana laughs. "Go. I'll get it."

I leave her there, scooping up all my makeup and stuff.

I lock myself in a stall and let my head drop into my hands. I have to tell her. I have to. Maybe she'll understand and not hate me. And maybe ignorance is bliss.

After a few minutes, I flush the toilet and push through

the door. As I weave through a bunch of people who are gyrating to the music, a girl grabs my hand and spins me under her arm. I almost say, I'm not available. I'm in love.

But at that moment Liana's eyes meet mine across the room. She's not smiling; in fact, her expression is scaring me.

That's when I see it. Swan's cell. In Liana's hand.

I hustle back and say, "I can explain."

Her eyes are black as coal.

I sit on the edge of the sofa.

"How long have you had this?" she says.

I want to lie so badly, but the time for truth has arrived. "I found it in Swan's room the day of the funeral...."

She blinks in horror. Shooting to her feet, she tosses the cell on the sofa, where it bounces to the floor. She snags her bag and heads for the exit.

I run out after her. "Liana, please! Let me explain."

She sprints up the stairs.

"I admit I sent the texts because I didn't know who you were and I didn't want to call you because I didn't think you should find out over the phone."

At the front door, she whirls. "You lied to me. All this time you could've told me you were the one who sent the texts, but you didn't."

I open my mouth to explain further, but there is no explanation. A lie of omission is still a lie.

She pushes out the door and trots to her car.

"Liana, wait!" I chase her down. "I wasn't thinking how it would affect you. Please. You have to believe me."

She climbs into her car, backs up, and speeds out of the

lot, running the stop sign on Colfax and almost T-boning a truck. The driver lays on his horn.

Tears roll down my cheeks and I stand there, trying to catch my breath. No. No no no.

"Hey," a voice says at my side. "You forgot your things." It's the girl who swung me under her arm. She's gathered all my junk from the floor and sofa, including Swanee's phone.

I can't even move my arm to take it from her. She tilts her head at me. "Are you okay?"

Okay? Okay? I don't even know the meaning of the word.

Chapter 23

All day Sunday I wait for my cell to ring. I know it won't. And I can't bring myself to call her. No apology would be enough to restore her trust in me.

On the drive home last night the cabdriver kept asking if there was anything he could do, since I was having a total meltdown, and I almost told him to hit a lamppost and put me out of my misery. But that would only create a ripple effect of misery for my parents and his family, if he had any.

Why didn't I throw away that cell phone? After falling for Liana, I didn't need a tether to Swanee anymore.

The house is so quiet, and my heart aches so much, that I need to go somewhere, do something to find solace. I don't know why my feet lead me to Ethan's room.

He's asleep, his origami-crane mobile dangling above his crib. I made it for him the day before he came home from the hospital. I read that cranes represent honor, loyalty, and peace, and are used to celebrate special occasions, like births and weddings. As far as honor and loyalty go, I'll never find lasting love, or get married. I'll never have a baby.

Ethan twitches his arms and legs, and his eyeballs move behind his eyelids. He must be dreaming. I wonder what babies dream, if they have fantasies or nightmares. Their life experience is so limited—how could they have that much to dream about? Unless people are reincarnated, which means we might have memories from hundreds of lives lived before ours.

God, I hope my previous lives were happier than this one.

I beg off Sunday with the family by telling Mom I'm not feeling well. At least it's not a lie.

When I trudge down for breakfast on Monday, Dad asks, "How was your date?"

The absolute wrong question. I burst into tears.

No way am I going to make it through a school day. I run upstairs and shut myself in my room. After a while, someone knocks. It takes every ounce of willpower I have not to growl, Go away.

The door opens and I cocoon myself in my sheet and blanket, feigning whatever fatal and contagious disease is currently at the top of the charts.

A weight drops on the bed.

"Do you want to talk about it?" Mom asks quietly.

I don't. I really, really don't. She touches my head and I roll over, digging my face into Mom's lap, and bawl like a baby. She brushes my hair over my ear, resting her head on mine. "I'm a good listener," she says.

In sobs and hiccups I relate the whole humiliating episode of finding Swanee's cell and texting Liana, meeting her, betraying her trust. "When she found out what a terrible person I am, she broke up with me."

Mom clicks her tongue. "If that's the worst thing you ever do in your life, I'm nominating you for sainthood." Which makes me cry harder, because aren't all the saints Catholic?

To her credit, Mom doesn't offer platitudes, like Give it time. Or This, too, will pass.

Because it won't.

Mom's beeper goes off and she checks it.

I roll off her.

She says, for the first time I can remember, "It can wait."

I take a few deep breaths to calm myself. "Can I skip school today?" And every day after?

She nods. "I'll call in."

While she's in sympathetic mode, I ask, "Can I buzz-cut my hair?"

She makes a face. "No."

Damn.

It's useless lying in bed. It only makes me relive the past and hate myself for what I did. Tuesday, on my way to school, I wait behind the juniper bush at the end of the cul-de-sac for Joss. Finally, ten minutes after the bell would've rung, I see her plodding down the sidewalk, head down. Her hair is stringy and greasy, and she has the same expression on her face she always wears: dead girl walking.

"Joss." I step out from behind the bush. "I have something for you," I tell her. I remove Swanee's cell from my pocket. "Jewell's probably cut off the service, and the cover doesn't glow anymore, but I know how much you want it."

Joss looks from the phone to me.

"I found it in the hospital bag in her room."

"When?"

"The day of the service."

"You stole it."

Yes! Okay? I stole it!

"You're a thief and a liar," she says.

"You're right. I'm sorry. I should've given it to you right away." How many lives have been affected by the things I should've done differently?

Joss is no dummy. "You're the one who was texting Liana. Is that how you hooked up?"

"We didn't mean to."

She shakes her head.

"I swear. Anyway, it doesn't matter, because we broke up."

She raises her eyebrows a little. "Why? You were the perfect couple: a liar and a skank."

"Don't blame Liana. She didn't know. I'm the one who betrayed her."

Joss says, "There's a lot of that going around."

I think she's coming to realize how Swanee took advantage of her. "Joss, you have to talk to someone about Swan's death. If not me, then a counselor. Or your parents."

"Talk to *you*? The person who used Swan to find a new girlfriend? I'm so sure." She brushes by me, almost knocking me off the sidewalk.

I call out, "At least take the brochures. There are lots of resources in the back."

Joss says over her shoulder, "You read the fucking brochures. You need more help than I do."

She may be right. I can't be trusted with anybody's heart.

I need to get rid of this cell phone. Every person it's touched has been burned. I return home and ask Dad if I can borrow the car for about an hour. He says, "Aren't you late for school?"

"Yeah. But I need to do something first." Please don't ask what.

"Okay," he says.

I grab the keys and toss my bag into the front seat of the car. At Stanley Lake, I park in the lot and retrieve Swanee's phone from my bag. The ice has melted, and geese are grazing along the shoreline. They hiss at me as I walk through a gaggle of them, and if I weren't on a mission I might find them intimidating. Stretching back as far as possible, I fling the cell into the lake, where it lands a few hundred yards away. I wish I had a better pitching arm, so it'd sink in the middle and never be found again. My best hope is that they don't dredge this lake, or that a drought doesn't suck up the shallows.

"Why, Swanee?" I ask aloud. "Why did you feel it was necessary to cheat on us? I loved you, Liana loved you. I bet Rachel did, too. Why wasn't that enough? I got what I deserved by lying to Liana." My voice breaks. "Not that you deserved to die. But if you're looking down on your life, you can't be very proud of how you lived it." I pause to take a deep breath. "Wherever you are, I hope you're asking for forgiveness and redemption. Because I am."

* * *

Losing Liana is even worse than Swanee's death, and I don't think it's because the pain is compounded. I feel so depressed that I don't even have the energy to begin my homework. My head feels as heavy as lead and drops to my pack.

My eyes catch the edges of the brochures sticking out of the front pocket. I retrieve the first one and read the title again: "The Five Stages of Grief." I open it.

Denial, anger, bargaining, depression, and acceptance, not necessarily in that order. I can see where I went through each stage with Swanee, even bargaining with a God I'm not sure I believe in to bring her back.

Where am I with Liana? Depressed. Angry at myself for being so stupid. Accepting of the fact that she has every reason in the world to never want to see me again.

A week goes by, and then two, with no calls or texts from Liana, not that I expect her to contact me. One night after everyone's gone to bed I log on to Facebook and see that she's unfriended me. Again.

I sit for an hour building up courage. Then I text her:

I'm sorry. Forgive me. I love you

I go to press Send, and then stop. I don't deserve to be forgiven. I don't deserve to be loved.

I end the call.

Spring is usually my favorite season of the year, with all the tulips and daffodils and crab apple trees in bloom. This year, though, there's a haze that clings to the air, dulling all the colors. The only bright moment is when I get my critical analysis paper back and see that Mrs. Burke gave me an

A. But then I'm sad again, because watching *Little Miss Sunshine* reminds me of kissing Liana.

One Saturday morning in April, Dad catches me after I've finished cleaning up from breakfast. "What are you doing this morning?" He's in the living room, rubbing Ethan's gum where his new tooth is coming in. We've counted five teeth so far, so this'll make six.

"I don't know. I thought I'd watch toons on TV with you guys."

"Let's take a drive." He lifts Ethan and drapes him over his shoulder.

"Where to?"

He doesn't answer as he jogs upstairs. A few minutes later he's back and Ethan's dressed—in the same jean overalls and striped shirt that Liana picked out for him. It's like déjà vu, where everything I see and touch and taste and smell reminds me of her.

Dad says, "Will you put Ethan in the car seat while I call your mom?"

Ethan's a happy boy, smiling and playing with his toys. He's started crawling, and his vocabulary's growing every day. He even has a name for me that sounds like "seesee," for *Sissy.*

Dad gets in the driver's seat and we both strap into our seat belts. He still hasn't told me where we're going. I suspect it's someplace really exciting, like OfficeMax or Safeway.

I must be lost in thought because I barely notice when the car pulls into a lot and stops.

"Where are we?" I ask.

Dad cocks his head. "You really do need glasses."

The enormous sign smacks me in the face: LAKEWOOD FORDLAND.

Dad gets out and detaches Ethan's carrier from the car seat. He starts toward the entrance, and then turns and sees that I'm still sitting in the car. "Are you coming?"

I guess I'm coming.

I follow Dad into the showroom, where he's immediately ambushed by a salesman. "Good morning. What can we do for you today?" the salesman asks.

Dad says, "We're here to buy a car."

He didn't tell me they were buying a new car.

Dad adds, "For my daughter."

What?

The salesman smiles at me. "What's the occasion?"

Hell if I know.

"She's earned it," Dad says.

I have?

"Do you have a particular model in mind? I'm Bob, by the way." He extends his hand to shake ours.

Dad hands Ethan's carrier to me and pulls out a fistful of papers. "I've done some research," he says, "and it looks like the Ford Focus is a good choice." He goes on about safety rating and price and value and blah, blah. "It'll have to be used. If that's okay with you, Alix."

Okay? I'd take a Go Kart at this point.

The front door opens and Mom rushes in. Another salesperson attacks her, but she says, "I'm with them." She catches up to us and asks, "Did I miss it?"

Dad glances over at me. "No. I think she's still exhibiting signs of shock and awe."

Mom smiles and takes the baby from me. As we trail Bob out into the lot, Dad babbles on about all the cars he found online that seem suitable, and keeps asking me if I'm good with that, and all I can do is nod my head yes yes yes.

The first car we stop at is a red Ford Focus hatchback. Bob pitches the slew of features and the pristine condition, but all I can see is the color.

"Alix?" Dad says. "What do you think?"

"Not red."

"Okay." He sorts through his papers and moves all the red cars to the back.

Bob shows us this black hatchback, which he calls Tuxedo Black. Again with all the features. It looks pretty cool. "Do you like it?" he asks me.

"I guess."

"Want to take it out for a spin?"

As in, drive it? I look to Mom, and then Dad. Everyone's waiting for my answer. "Sure."

"Let me go get the keys," Bob says.

It looks brand-new, but Dad tells me it's two years old. He reads the online report and informs us it only has a little over ten thousand miles. Bob comes back with the key and opens the driver's side for me.

"You do have your license, right?" Mom asks. To Dad she says, "Did you make sure she brought her license?"

"Oops."

"I have it," I say. I don't go anywhere without it, just in case my parents decide to buy me a car. Right?

Bob slides in on the passenger side and I sit there waiting for Mom and Dad to climb in the back. When I realize they're not going to, I tune in to all the features and functions Bob is rattling off. He says, "It's a stick. Do you know how to drive a stick?"

"I've driven Mom's Forester a few times." Like twice, since it scares the bejeezus out of me. "It's a stick." With six speeds that I never have been able to navigate. When I go to put the car into reverse, though, I grind the gear. I wince and he says, "You always have to get used to different cars."

That makes me feel better. He instructs me to head toward Sixth Avenue so I can see how it feels on the highway. My whole body is shaking and I'm gripping the steering wheel so hard my knuckles are white. I manage to merge into traffic without killing anyone and finally take a breath. Someone honks at me and zips around my left side to pass. "You might want to speed up just a little," Bob says, and smiles.

My eyes dart up and down, up and down, and I finally find the speedometer. I'm going forty in a sixty-five-miles-per-hour zone. When we get to Wadsworth, Bob says, "You can exit here if you want."

I want. He directs me back to the dealership on side streets to show me how it handles in the city. When we pull into the dealership, Mom and Dad are sitting outside on a bench with Ethan between them in his carrier. They get up and walk toward us as I pull into a parking space.

"Well?" Dad says.

"I'll take it."

Dad laughs.

"What?"

"I think you should drive more than one before you decide."

That only increases the odds I'll add to the toll of teenage accidents and/or road rage incidents. Numbly, I follow Bob as he shows me a white car (boring), and then a silver one. My eyes stray to the one next to the silver car. "What about that one?" I ask.

It's metallic blue and not a hatchback. Sleek, and more sporty. Dad riffles through his papers and says, "I don't have any research on it."

"It just came in yesterday," Bob informs us. "Three years old, but it only has eight thousand miles."

"Wow," Dad says. He asks all kinds of questions about the safety inspection and Blue Book value, while I run my hand along the hood and look inside. It has a white leather interior. Not very practical, Mom would say, but since this is my car, practical doesn't play into the decision.

"Can I take it out?" I say before Bob even asks.

He looks at Dad and Dad shrugs. "She's the customer."

Oh my God. Dad was right about driving more than one. This one is so much better. It feels solid and steady in my hands, like it was meant to be. I don't even want to go back to the dealership; I want to just keep driving and never look back.

Bob jolts me out of my reverie by asking, "Are we headed to Vegas? Because I should probably call my wife."

He winks at me, not in a perverted kind of way, but a jokester-guy way.

When we get back, I tell Mom and Dad, "This is definitely the one."

"If you're sure," Dad says.

"I'm positive."

Dad says to Bob, "Write 'er up."

As we're walking into the showroom, I ask, "Is this going on my Visa, which I'll never be able to pay back in a million years?"

Mom looks at Dad and they both crack up. Mom links her arm in mine. "This one's on us."

Chapter 24

As soon as all the paperwork is done, I ask Mom and Dad if I can take a drive. Dad replies, "I don't know how else we're going to get the car home, unless they're handing out driver's licenses to nine-month-old babies now." He adds in a mutter, "Wouldn't surprise me."

I know the first place I'm going. Ten minutes later, when I pull to the curb, she's just getting out of her car. She's wearing her uniform.

We both stand for a minute and look at each other. I know she hates me, and there's no excuse for my behavior, and even if there was, she might not accept my apology. But I have to try.

"Hi." I approach her.

At least she doesn't run away.

"How are you?" I ask.

"Good," she says. "And you?" Kind of icy.

The conversation stalls. "I got a new car," I say. "Well, it's used."

She peers around me. "Nice."

"That's not what I came to say. I wanted to tell you I'm sorry. I'm sorry about everything that went down. I cherish your friendship, and I'd never do anything to hurt you, and I know I did and if there's any way I can make it up to you, I want to because I miss you and need you in my life." I'm choking and tears are filling my eyes.

Betheny crosses the lawn and puts her arms around me. "I'm sorry, too. For months I've tried to figure out ways to say how sorry I was about Swanee, but you didn't seem to really want to talk about it."

"I know."

"It must've been incredibly hard for you."

She doesn't know the half of it. I burst into full-blown tears, and she lets me cry it out on her shoulder. "So, are we okay again?" she asks.

"We are so okay."

She hugs me and I hug her back. When she lets me go, she shrieks at the top of her lungs, "You got a car!"

We leap into the air together and high-five.

She puts her hands onto her hips and goes, "Are you even going to offer me a ride?"

"If you have a death wish, get in."

The rain starts as a drizzle on Thursday, and by Friday it's a monsoon. But guess what? I have a car to drive home from school! As I'm changing from my school clothes into sweats, listening to the rain spatter against my windows, I remember the party Swanee took me to the first weekend after our ski trip. There was a really great DJ and I could've danced the whole time. But Swanee wanted to get stoned, so that's what we did.

In my memory, her face morphs into Liana's and I think, We never even got to dance. She'd probably dance circles around me, and we'd lose ourselves in the music and in each other.

I feel a catch in my throat and swallow it down. Forget feeling sorry for myself. That isn't even one of the five stages of grief.

Downstairs, Mom's stirring a vat of chili.

"Smells yummy," I tell her, snaking my arms around her waist.

"If you want to help, you can slice the bread and butter it," she says.

As soon as I saw off the heel of the bread, the doorbell rings. Mom sets down her spoon and says, "I'll get it."

I hear the door open, and then silence. Mom says, "You're sopping wet. Come in. It's for you, Alix," she calls.

Joss always picks the worst times, I think.

I round the corner and stop dead.

Liana's in the foyer, drenched from head to toe.

Nothing—not a word—passes between us.

"Where's your car?" Mom glances over Liana's shoulder.

"It died," Liana says. To me, she adds, "I've been driving around the block for hours, and it ran out of gas."

Driving around doing what? I wonder.

"You're shivering," Mom says. "Alix, why don't you take Liana upstairs and get her into some dry clothes?"

That's not a good idea, I want to say. She might pound me into dog meat.

Mom asks her, "Do you want to stay for dinner? There's plenty."

"No," I snap at Mom. Liana's suffered enough pain at my hands.

Mom ignores me.

Liana says, "That's okay. I don't want to put you out. I just wanted to talk to Alix."

About what?

"It's no problem," Mom says. "I always make enough to feed us for a month."

Liana holds my eyes.

Why is Mom doing this? Torturing her, and me?

Once we cross the threshold of my room, Liana shuts the door behind her. She shoves me onto the bed and plops beside me, sitting on one bent leg. "True or false," she says. "If I hadn't met you, I never would've learned about Swan's lies."

"You might have eventually."

"How? Who was going to tell me? You're the only one who was even considerate enough to think I might want to know she was dead. Question two: true or false. I never would've gotten my ring back if it wasn't for you."

"Jewell might've found it when she was cleaning out the room." Except I doubt Jewell knew about the ring if Joss didn't.

"The answer's true," Liana says. She goes on, "If we hadn't gone through this the way we did, I never would've gotten to use another forgiveness chip with God. Every one I trade in gets me closer to heaven."

She can't mean she forgives me.

She focuses on my face. "I wouldn't have met you and fallen in love."

I lower my eyes. "No. You would've met someone better. More honest. More trustworthy."

"Alix!" Her tone of voice jolts my head up. "How can I forgive you if you can't forgive yourself?"

I feel tears burning my eyes.

She scoots close, resting her forehead on mine. "I've missed you so much." She holds my face between her hands and kisses me.

I can't even speak to tell her how much I love and miss her.

It's like time has simply been suspended while I waited for this moment. We fall back on the bed and kiss until a knock sounds. Mom says through the door, "Dinner's ready."

"Shit." I bolt to a sitting position. "We'll be there in a minute."

"Should I set a place for you, Liana?" Mom asks.

I answer, "Yes, please."

Not only is Liana wet, but now my front is all damp. Mom's folded a stack of clean clothes for me to put away, so I dig out a pair of sweatpants and a sweatshirt for each of us. It's going to look suspicious that I've changed clothes, but I don't care. We both turn our backs to change.

Except I peek and see she's wearing a Victoria's Secret polka-dot bra. Goose bumps.

She's the same height as me, but my clothes look better on her. Sexy. Probably because she has more curves.

She gathers her pile of wet clothes and asks, "What do you want me to do with these?"

I take them from her. "I'll put them in the dryer during dinner. They should be ready by the time you leave." She clenches my free hand and that familiar tingle zaps me. "I can't believe this is happening. Pinch me," I say.

So she does. Hard enough for me to yelp.

Liana's manners are impeccable, of course. She compliments Mom on the chili and answers questions about her family. I learn that her mom works part-time at the post office and volunteers at church, and she tells them about her dad's research at UNC.

After dinner, Liana starts rinsing chili bowls in the sink.

"You two go," Dad says to us. "I'll take care of this."

Liana tells him, "I need to get a tow to a gas station. And call home, too, to let my mom and dad know where I am and that I'll be late." She adds, "I, uh, left my cell in the car, so would it be okay if I used your phone?"

Mom's beeper goes off. "It's still pouring out." She hurries over and lifts the phone from the cradle. "You shouldn't be driving in this weather, especially all the way to Greeley. Why don't you ask your parents if you can stay the night?"

Did that come from my mother's mouth? My. Mother?

Mom says, "We can take care of your car in the morning." Then she speaks into the phone: "What's up?"

Liana says to me, “I’m used to driving in bad weather.”

I overhear Mom say, “But she’s only at twenty-five weeks.” She listens, and then adds, “I’ll be there as fast as I can.” She races out of the room and up the stairs. Over the railing, she calls, “Alix, fix up the guest bedroom for Liana.”

“Feel free to use the phone,” Dad says at the same time.

Liana calls and explains the situation, and then says under her breath, “Papá…” She sighs. “Just a minute.” Handing the phone to Dad, she goes, “My dad wants to talk to you.”

I take Ethan from him, and Dad assures Liana’s father that she’s welcome to stay the night and tomorrow until the rain subsides, and then they talk about hydroplaning and splash back.

I say, “You want to see Ethan crawl?”

“Yeah.” She smiles. “He’s getting so big. It’s amazing what a difference twenty-seven days makes.”

She’s been counting the days?

Mom rushes through the kitchen, looking panicked.

“Good luck,” I call to her back. She doesn’t acknowledge it.

The dryer buzzes and Dad comes into the living room to relieve me of Ethan. As soon as I pull Liana’s clothes out, she’s beside me, taking them. “I really appreciate this, Alix,” she says.

I’d forgotten how big her eyes are, and how lustrous her hair. If Dad wasn’t within viewing range…

“The guest room is this way.” I wedge by her, my knees wobbly.

Our so-called guest room is mostly used for storage, so I start shoving boxes against the wall to find the bed. Liana helps, of course, and I wish I could tell her to just let me do it because every time she gets near, I'm tempted to throw her on the bed.

She must be feeling the same way because she presses me against the wall and smothers me in a deep kiss. In the doorway, Dad clears his throat, and I slither out of her arms.

"Let me finish rearranging," he says. "Alix, you go find sheets and blankets and a pillow." Do I detect a smile on his face?

After we're done preparing the room, Dad leaves to check on Ethan in his crib. All I want to do is shut the door, turn off the lights, and pick up where we left off.

Liana must read my mind or anticipate my move because she says, "I'm scared, Alix. I want you so badly, I don't think I could say no. Please understand."

I do.

"Plus, I'm exhausted," she says. "Would it be okay if I just went to bed?"

"Yeah, of course." I'm suddenly feeling drained, too. Pop quizzes do that to me. "Do you want some pj's?"

"Do you have a pair with bunnies or duckies?" she asks.

"No, but I have a merry widow."

She laughs. God, I've missed that laugh. "Do you have a long shirt or a nightgown?" she says.

Me, wear a nightgown? "Let me go get you a shirt."

Without warning, we hear a sound like bullets hitting the window, like machine-gun fire. We both duck down, covering our heads. Then we realize how dumb that looks and giggle. We go over to the window and gaze out. Rain is still sluicing down the glass, but now the ground is covered with pearls of ice. "It's hailing," we say in unison. She slugs me. "Owe me a Coke."

"Oh, man. I hope it doesn't dent my new car."

She turns to me. "You got a car?"

"For no reason, except maybe they were tired of me bugging them a hundred times a day."

"Or they felt you deserved it." She rests her head on my shoulder.

The hail is unrelenting. Now I really am worried about my car. "Hopefully, Dad got me denters' insurance."

She twists to face me. "Is there such a thing?"

I just look at her. She wraps her hands around my neck and fake strangles me. She says, "I remember a couple of years ago we got this softball-sized hail. It didn't last too long, thank goodness, and afterward I went out and found the biggest chunk I could. It was actually a whole lot of little pieces of hail all globbed together. I put it in the freezer to keep forever. I wonder what happened to it."

I remember that storm, too. "Hang on," I say, and then sprint downstairs to the kitchen. At the back of the freezer is a Baggie, and I pull it out. I run back upstairs and show it to Liana.

Her eyes grow wide. She tosses me this lopsided smile and goes, "Great minds think alike."

Chapter 25

I hear Mom come in around two AM. I haven't been able to sleep, knowing Liana's just down the hall. Slipping out of bed, I go over and crack open my door. It startles Mom. "What are you doing up?" she whispers.

"Can't sleep. Is the baby okay?"

Mom's face tells the answer. I open my door all the way.

"We tried to stop the labor, but she had a placental abruption. The baby weighed just over a pound, and we kept him alive for six hours. But his lungs were severely underdeveloped, and he had a heart defect. Then his brain began to hemorrhage. Poor little thing."

I go over and hug Mom around the waist. It's tragic. Dying young, at any age.

Mom says, "At least we saved the mom. I'm wiped. I need to go to bed." She unlocks my arms from behind her and plants a kiss on my head.

I return to my room, and a minute later a soft knock

sounds on the door. I get up to answer it. Liana's there, her arms folded across her chest.

"Did the baby make it?" she asks.

I shake my head.

Her face falls. I hear Mom and Dad talking in their room, so I pull Liana into mine and shut the door.

"I can't sleep," she says.

"Me neither." In the glow of my digital alarm, all I can see is her silhouette, but it brings me to full alert. "You want to watch a movie on my iPad?"

"Sure," she goes.

She trails me to my desk, and when I stop abruptly, she runs into me. She giggles. It makes me want to laugh, too, but I suppress it.

"Did you close your door? Because if my mom or dad knows you're in here with me..."

We both pad to the door and peek out to make sure the coast is clear.

"Be right back," Liana whispers. She tiptoes down the hall, closes her door quietly, and then tiptoes back.

There's only one chair at my desk, but we could sit on the floor, or the bed. She says, "I promise to keep my hands and lips to myself if you do."

I raise a palm. "Scout's honor."

She asks, "Were you ever a Scout?"

"Hell no."

She laughs, and then claps a hand over her mouth.

I place the iPad between us as she hops into bed beside me. As we're scrolling through movies, I ask her, "Do you think it's harder to lose a baby who's only been alive for six hours, or a person who's a little older? Say, seventeen. Someone who's left a mark." Even if it was scuff marks on others' hearts.

Liana doesn't answer for a long time. At last she says, "I don't think it matters. You either love your children or you don't. They'll always be a part of you."

I wasn't talking about parents. I meant me. Her.

"Let me know if you see something you like." I'm on the third or fourth page of movies before I realize her eyes are locked on me.

"What?"

"I see something I like." She takes the iPad, leans across me, and sets it on the nightstand. Hovering over me, she lowers her head and kisses me, gently at first, and then more passionately. I know I should turn away, tell her to stop, but I can't. I want her.

She takes me in her arms and rolls me to the side to face her. "I lied," she says.

"Me too."

I close my eyes and we're kissing again. Then, just as quickly as we started, we stop. Liana throws an arm over me and we just cuddle. Talk.

"Can I ask you a question?" I say.

"Ask me anything. I don't want us to ever keep secrets, Alix."

"Cross my heart and hope to—"

She grabs my hand and presses it to her heart. "Live."

"Live." Although that promise is up to fate.

"What's your question?" she asks.

"It's about your religion," I say. "I don't want to offend you."

"You won't. What do you want to know?"

"Do you ever think it's hypocritical to be Catholic, knowing that they condemn gay people?"

As soon as the words are out, I wish I could take them back. She has the right to believe whatever she wants.

"You're right," she says. "It's hard to rationalize how a person can buy into some of the teachings of a religion and not others. All I know is that I love God, and believing there's a higher power and a heaven to go to when you die gives me comfort. There are a lot of teachings I don't believe. Like you can't practice birth control; you can only go to a Catholic church; you can't wear polyester."

"What? Seriously?"

"For me, though, God is love, pure and simple. And God would never ask me to choose between my truth and my faith."

That makes sense to me. I could build a personal spirituality based on love.

"Did I answer your question?" Liana asks.

"Yes. Thanks."

"You're welcome." She runs the backs of her fingers down my face and kisses me. We don't go any further than kissing. Touching. She's soft and warm and safe. I think safe is what we both need right now.

Bright sunshine streaks through the curtains and my bleary eyes drift across the bed. She's still here, spooning against me.

I glance at my clock and gasp. Ten thirty? "Liana." I shake her shoulder a little.

She murmurs.

"You have to go back to the guest room." If Mom or Dad finds us here...

"But I don't want to." She links a leg in mine and rolls me over. She rakes her fingers through my hair.

Liana must hear the footsteps on the stairs at the same time I do. She scrambles to untangle herself from the sheet.

At that moment, a knock sounds and my door opens. Mom sticks her head in. "I need you to run some errands for me, if you don't mind."

"I don't mind." Glancing sideways across the bed, I notice Liana's not visible. She must've leapt off the mattress just in time.

Mom adds, "Good morning, Liana. Maybe on the way Alix can fill a gas can so you can get your car to a station."

"Okay," this tiny voice squeaks from the floor. "Thanks."

Mom leaves and I sprawl across the bed. Liana's flat on her stomach, her butt cheeks fully exposed around her thong.

"Hold on." I grab my iPad. "Let me get a shot of this for Facebook."

Epilogue

I see Joss a few times at school, but whenever our eyes meet she turns and bolts. I get the message. I'm her worst memory of her dead sister. One day I drive by her cul-de-sac and there's a FOR SALE sign stuck in the Durbins' front yard with a SOLD banner slapped across it. My first thought is, I hope wherever Joss lands, she'll make a new beginning for herself.

The distance between Arvada and Greeley is still a pain, but school's out for both of us, so Liana and I have more time to spend together. Our girls' track team went to the state finals, even without Swanee, and it was a blast cheering them on and hanging out with Betheny again. I'm pretty sure Swan wouldn't be pleased to know she wasn't as pivotal to the team as she thought. But in her short life, she did find her passion.

Liana suggested I set up a website to sell my jewelry. Her brother is studying to become a Web designer, and he agreed to help. "For a nominal fee," he told Liana. Liana told him,

"'Nominal' meaning 'free.'" She threatened to rat him out about his speeding tickets, and now I've got a very cool website called Bejeweled by Alixandra. In the first week, I actually sold two sets of earrings. It's awesome imagining my jewelry being worn by people who find it beautiful or funky. I'm applying to CU to study art. Or premed. Or both. Liana's going to need a roommate. Right?

Liana and I are meeting at Red Rocks Amphitheatre for the July 4 concert and fireworks display. Even though we're officially a couple now, prior to the concert, we wanted to finalize one aspect of our lives so it wouldn't always be hanging over us.

As I turn into the entrance for Red Rocks, I see that Liana's car is already in the lot, empty.

The sky is a dazzling blue against the white helium-filled balloon I bought at Party City on my way here. The balloon bobs in the breeze as I make my way up the trail to the auditorium. I don't want to lose my balloon in the wind, so I wrap the ribbons three times around my wrist.

Liana's sitting on the top riser with her white balloon, and when she sees me she stands and waves. I hurry to her and we embrace. "You're late," she says. "Did you have trouble finding it?"

"Yeah. My GPS is permanently set on Greeley." We laugh. If you live in Colorado, you know where Red Rocks Amphitheatre is. Not to mention I'm fifteen minutes early.

"Are you ready?" she asks me.

"In a minute. I wrote something." I fish in the front

pocket of my shorts and pull out a sheet of paper folded in fourths. If there's one thing I've learned through all of this, thanks to both Swanee and Liana, it's that we have so little control over what happens to us in life. But we do have the power to forgive, both ourselves and others.

"It's not that good," I say to Liana.

"If you wrote it, it's Pulitzer Prize material."

I snort. "Hold this." I hand her my white balloon.

We sit, both of us gazing down at the empty stage. We considered doing this at Jeffco Stadium, where Swan died, but agreed that would be morbid. And melancholy is not our intent today.

"Ready?" I say.

"Could you be any more dramatic?"

"Shut up."

She grins. Her hair glistens in the sun and a curly tendril blows into her mouth. I reach over and brush it away.

Unfolding the paper, I take a deep breath and recite:

"Maybe you knew
how short your time would be
how your love
could be potent
possessive
poison.
We loved the person
we knew
or thought we did.
That'll never change.

Love can give you life
or take it away
you can pass it on
or stop it in its tracks."

I hesitate. "Is it awful?"

"No. But it feels unfinished."

"Duh. Because there's more." I continue:

"We want you to know
we forgive you
and we thank you
for bringing us together."

I refold the paper. "That's it."

Liana takes my hand and squeezes. "It's perfect. Now are you ready?"

I nod.

She hands me back my balloon. We discussed buying a bunch of multicolored balloons, but decided in the end on the two white ones, symbolizing doves. Peace and serenity. We couldn't abandon the rainbow completely, so we each got a variety of colored ribbons tied to the ends of the balloons. We knot all the ribbons together and stand up.

Our fingers curl together around the knot and I say, "On the count of three."

We count, "One, two, three," and then release both balloons. They rise into the air, the ribbons fluttering like kite tails. Liana and I shade our eyes and watch as a gust of wind whips the balloons down the auditorium, between the red granite towers, over the stage, and out of sight.

Liana and I snake our arms around each other, resting our temples together. Then we kiss. Liana breaks free and points straight up in the sky. I catch a final glimpse of our balloons, sailing high into the heavens.

Good-bye, Swanee, I say to myself. You were my first, and that'll never change. But life goes on, and so do survivors. Liana and I are joining their ranks.

Acknowledgments

None of my crazy career choices would've been possible without the enduring love and encouragement of my partner, Sherri Leggett.

When I told her, "I quit my (very high-paying tech) job today to become a writer," she said, "Ho-kay. Have you ever written anything?"

I said, "Pfft. No. But look at all the books out there. How hard can it be?"

I'm here to tell you, it's haaaaaaaaaaaaaaaard.

I owe my twenty-five-year writing career to my editor, Megan Tingley, who discovered me while we were still in trainers. She's been my mentor from the time she was an associate editor until now, in her current position as Executive Vice President and Publisher at Little, Brown Books for Young Readers. I've brought her a long way, don't you think? Thank you, too, to all the employees at LBYR who work their butts off to make great books.

Not long after Megan and I met, it was my great fortune to hook up (figuratively) with my brilliant agent, Wendy Schmalz. She's been my biggest champion and will remain my friend forever and ever. That woman can work miracles.

An author needs support from her writing community, and I am extremely grateful to The Wild Writers (thewild writers.com) for their time and talents in critiquing my work.

Thank you to all the teachers and librarians who make my books available to young readers, and to the readers themselves, young and young-at-heart, who've continued my cycle of empowerment by letting me know how much my books have validated, comforted, and inspired them.

Adopt a cat today.

Love, Julie

PROVOCATIVE, HEART-WRENCHING, HOPEFUL...

Read all of award-winning author JULIE ANNE PETERS's inspiring novels:

Define "Normal"
Keeping You a Secret
Luna
Pretend You Love Me
She Loves You, She Loves You Not...
It's Our Prom (So Deal With It)

• • • • • • •

JULIE ANNE PETERS lives with her partner, Sherri Leggett, in Lakewood, Colorado.